Diary of a WALLFLOWER

First Published in Great Britain in 2019 by
LOVE AFRICA PRESS
103 Reaver House, 12 East Street, Epsom KT17 1HX
www.loveafricapress.com

ACKNOWLEDGEMENTS

This book would not have been possible if not for my pastor who had said 'You say you want to be a writer, write on Facebook and let's see if people like your stories.' That was the push that started it all. Thank you, Mr. Michael Ndekwu.

To Kiru Taye, Zee Monodee and Love Africa Press, I say thank you for believing in this story and for your incredible platform that has afforded African romance to shine into the world.

My mom, dad and siblings have been a constant source of support, never looking at me weird when I go off for hours into fantasyland and emerge like a zombie into the real world. Thank you for looking away when I laughed to myself and didn't regard me as mad.

I would not forget my late uncle, Leo Agbor, the man who had introduced me to books and reading. His love for newspapers and that big old library in his house opened a whole new world for me that enabled me to dream. You are not forgotten.

To my earliest loyal readers, Destiny Madubuike, Sophia Asuru, Ifeoma Ndewku, Faith Martins, and all my friends on Facebook, your enthusiasm for my stories made this possible.

To my incredible readers, I say thank you. This journey has just begun.

DEDICATION

This book is dedicated to my Lord and Saviour Jesus, who had loved me despite my imperfections.

To every wallflower out there, you will bloom and the world will bow.

Dear Diary,

I don't really know how to do this; I've never had a diary before, even as a teenager. You're supposed to be confidential, so I know my secrets are safe with you, right?

Well, my name is Glory Owhor, and the most interesting thing about me is how I know ten different delicious ways to make spaghetti. That's it. I'm boring, really boring. I am a typical Nigerian church girl, a dry, bland wallflower—I am literally obsessed with Jesus, so I am always in church whenever I can. I have no life outside work, church, and home. It's my routine day in, day out, every month, year by year.

God! Even I am so freaking tired of it.

Oh. Another interesting thing about me—I use a lot of swear words, but only in my head. I mean, I never use really offensive words like the '*f*' word or the '*a*' word, but still, it's really bad. And I take the name of the Lord our God in vain a lot (Again, only inside my head.). I don't drink, go to bars, or go clubbing. Heck, I can't remember the last time I went on a date. And yes, you guessed it right. I am a virgin, a freaking virgin in this age and time. How did it happen?

Well, let's just say I have been accused of been a prude and a stuck-up, emotionally dead person. Mostly by angry boyfriends who get offended when they can't get the cookie. I have heard it so much, I'm beginning to think it's true.

It's just, truthfully, I am tired of being Miss Goody Two Shoes all the freaking time. I want to experience things, do things, go crazy, have fun now I am still young. Being an uptight prude has brought me nothing but loneliness. A single working girl in Nigeria is sometimes, a lonely one. My mom has been on my case to get married, but here I sit, day in, day out, not interested in any guy at all. What is wrong with me?

Did I tell you I think a lot, too? That's why I'm telling you all this. My friend Simon gave you to me as a birthday gift last year, and you've just been sitting in my pile of books, gathering dust, but suddenly, I have all these thoughts running riot in my head, and I need a place to vent before I go crazy.

Anyways, my boring life is practically stifling me, but out of the blue, something interesting has happened, and this is what I want to tell you.

This is not a romance or a love story, so prepare to be disappointed. In fact, I am not proud of some of the things I have done, but you can't judge me, okay?

PART ONE
It Begins

CHAPTER ONE

Now you are older and more experienced, what have you done with it?

This was the voice echoing in my head during the impromptu rehearsals that Friday evening. The text had come in the morning, asking all choir members to be in church by five p.m., and though I wasn't particularly feeling tired, I just couldn't concentrate. Simon, the music director, was waving his hands wildly and jumping up and down as he tried to explain some things to the whole choir unit. He was always like this, very passionate about his music. And even though he definitely noticed me paying very little attention or singing with a focused mind, he didn't reprimand me. Simon is my friend, almost my best friend if not for his gender.

While the choir rehearsed with all their heart and gusto, some sweating profusely as their veins strained for their voice to hit the high notes, my mind was far away, in a land of dejection. I just wasn't happy. I couldn't bring myself to smile. Lately, my life has been feeling like old okra soup, unwanted and boring, tasteless and kind of annoying. What am I doing here, sef? What is the point of all this? Why couldn't I just feel satisfied?

My heart, my body, my soul have been yearning, searching for something deeper, something to add colour to my dreary life, something to make my heart beat again. This couldn't be all there was to life. There had to be something more. What is it? Why can't I find it?

I don't even know what I'm searching for. I don't know what my body, my heart, misses. I feel like I'm missing somebody, a stranger maybe, something I have never had before.

Love, maybe?

Hormonal clock ticking?

Lord, why do I feel this way? I'm thankful for everything I have in my life right now. Please, help me to find peace again, to be content.

I prayed silently in my heart, tears filling my eyes. Great! Now the whole choir unit will want to know the reason for my tears. How can I explain something I don't even understand?

I stood up hastily, raised my finger up as Simon turned to me in urgency, and walked outside, towards the generator house humming softly. Even if I cried here, nobody would hear me. The generator would mask any noise I make.

But the tears didn't come again, just a silent rage inside me that kept building up. I closed my fist tightly, wondering why I wanted so badly to hit something, anything.

"What is it?"

Simon stood beside me.

That was all it took. The tears appeared again, lodging in my chest like a wave as I struggle to hold it in. Still, they fell, cascading down my cheeks even as I shook my head in the negative to Simon, a small squeaky sound escaping from my throat like the mews of a small puppy.

Simon smiled and hugged me tight. I didn't have an answer for my tears. They just came, pouring faster and faster.

The sound of footsteps echoed around. Someone was coming. Even if we are innocent, it wouldn't be nice for anyone to see us in the dark like this on church premises. I let go of his shirt and stood up straight, cleaning my eyes with the scented handkerchief he'd pulled out of his pocket.

"Let's go inside. We'll just say the final prayer and close," he said.

We went back in. A buzz, an excitement, hummed in the air. Everyone was straightening their hair and jackets, prepping for something.

"Pastor Lanre has come," somebody whispered to Simon.

The senior pastor? He didn't usually attend any of our rehearsals. What could he possibly want with us?

Simon hurried outside, showing no surprise. This must be the reason he had called for the rehearsals. Pastor Lanre had wanted to see the choir before our usual rehearsal day, Saturday.

The last time he came to our rehearsal, it was to drop a bombshell. Oh, God! Not another scandal, please. We have barely recovered from the last one.

Two months ago, Pastor Lanre suspended two of our choir members for engaging in fornication. We all fasted and prayed for days not just for God's forgiveness, but for grace to overcome temptations. Don't roll your eyes at me, diary. I know, in this age and time, these things still happen, especially if you're caught in it as a prominent member of the Christian faith. Choir members are supposed to be role models, right? Anyways, these ones came out publicly, and I'm talking about pregnancy here, so it had to be punished.

Already, I haven't been happy since that incident. If something similar happened again, it would put the spiritual lives of the choir members in doubt. *Oh, God, please help us to be holy*. I made a sign of the cross unconsciously, something I had picked up from my days attending mass in secondary school, and hurried to my seat. Bianca and Chioma, my friends seated beside me, held my hands tight as we made a small prayer of agreement amongst ourselves.

"Don't worry. Nothing like that will happen again!" Chioma assured me.

My smile couldn't hide my nerves. I know what you're thinking. We're all a bunch of holy, sanctimonious people, right? Well, this is something we have committed our lives to, so try to understand.

Simon cleared his throat loudly and stood aside, ushering in Pastor Lanre. I smiled in spite of myself. There is just something about the senior pastor that makes everyone smile. He is friendly, gentle, and caring, yet firm and rigid when it comes to the standard of God. He is just fifty-five, with four grown children, yet he looked handsome and young like a man in his forties.

He smiled, reducing the tension in the room. If he was smiling, it couldn't be bad news.

"Good evening, everyone..." he began.

"Good evening, sir," the choir unit responded.

The drummer rolled his sticks and banged on the drum, making Pastor Lanre smile widely and point to him.

"Kelechi, I know you're excited. Try to contain yourself."

"Yes, sir!" Kelechi thundered, standing up and stomping his feet in salute.

Everyone laughed.

"Okay! Before anyone else gets any ideas, I just came to inform you that somebody will give a special number on Sunday. No, you don't know him. He just flew into the country, and he'll be attending service on Sunday. So, Simon..." he called out to Simon, who rushed to his side. "Ensure the musicians learn this song, 'Make me Over' by Tyson Pierce, and get some back-up ready to assist him. Okay?"

"Okay, sir. Thank you, sir," Simon said, bowing slightly, his gaze already picking up some choir members to back-up the song.

I smiled and nodded slightly as his eyes landed on me.

Sometimes, Pastor Lanre invites guest pastors and/or singers, and he likes to get the choir ready for any song or ministration.

He left shortly after, and we said the final prayers and grace. Rehearsals were officially over. Simon called the few of us he had selected and sent the song to our phones.

"Learn it or die" he said sternly, his famous quote.

We laughed.

"Eh, Glory, are you still doing that song?"

Chioma came up to me as I left Simon.

"Which song?" I ask.

"The Kierra Sheard song."

I looked at her. She wanted to do the song. Chioma was such a song stealer.

"I know you just want to do the song. No wahala. Do it. I'll find another one. We'll see tomorrow," I said, hurrying to catch up with Simon.

He walked so fast, I only caught up with him as he got to his car.

"Have you finished?"

I nodded.

"Oya, let's go."

I got in, and he drove off. Simon's house is in my street. He usually drops me off Saturdays and Sundays.

I stayed quiet, not really thinking about anything.

"So ..." he started.

Great! He must want to know why I was crying earlier. I didn't even have an answer for him.

"Will you tell me why you were crying before?"

I shook my head. Why had I been crying? Discontentment? Ungratefulness? Who cried over nothing?

"I just don't know how to explain it. Lately, I've been feeling angry and discontent. You know, like my life has no meaning, like I'm not going anywhere. I'm just doing the same things every day."

Simon laughed.

I turn to glare at him. "It's not funny. I know I have no real reason, but I just can't shake this feeling away. Maybe I'm depressed."

He shook his head, still laughing. "You're not depressed, my dear. You're a child of Zion. We don't get depressed. Let me ask you, when was the last time you went anywhere except work and church?"

To be honest, I couldn't really remember.

"You see? That's why you're feeling like this. Besides, you've not had a boyfriend for about five years now, correct?"

I nod.

"See? That's why you're feeling discontent. Listen, Glory, I know you're born again, and it's why you don't want to date anybody right now."

"No, that's not it. I don't want to date. I want courtship with a husband-to-be. Tired of dating."

"In other words, you want to get married soon?" Simon asks.

Could my eyes boggle more in surprise as I turn to him? Was he crazy? What single, twenty-seven-year-old Nigerian girl was not thinking of getting married?

"No. I'm waiting 'til I get grey hair before I get married. It's just, I haven't really met anybody I am remotely interested in, so I'm just being patient. I even pray about it, but I get nothing."

Simon chuckled. "So what you're saying is God has not given you an answer. Must He?"

"Yes. I'm very serious about this. Just look at the rate of divorce these days. So many unhappy marriages everywhere."

"So if He gives you an answer, then you think everything will be rosy?"

"I know that even if God is involved, we'll still have to work hard to be together. But at least, I'll know God is the foundation. If anything funny wants to happen, I can just tell Him He should fix the man he gave me."

Simon laughed harder. "So you just want to blackmail God."

I smiled and shook my head.

He turned back to the road, his countenance now serious, and the news I had to share with him pops back into my head. "My new manager is starting tomorrow. I just hope it's not another lecherous old man like Mr. Bode"

My former boss, a randy old man, had been giving me thinly veiled threats for over a year. I don't know which was more repulsive—his pot belly, his white beard, or his dry, scaly skin that he would touch me with at any given opportunity.

Simon laughed again. "I know. So who's your new boss?"

"I don't know. The company is bringing someone who studied abroad. Imagine! As if Nigerian schools are useless."

"Ah! But you know the truth..." he began.

"What truth?" I counter. "Please, Nigerian schools also have standards. It's just the problem of bribery and a bad system that's killing us. And who told you these foreign schools don't have their own issues? There are also incidences of corruption rooted in their system. We are the ones who just feel like they're perfect. A foreign school graduate is not better than a Nigerian graduate. The only problem we have is strike, bribery, and badly qualified lecturers."

My arms were waving about to punctuate my point.

Simon frowned slightly. "Which is why they have the edge over us. So you're saying they should have given the job to somebody who schooled in Nigeria."

"Yes, if the person was more qualified and experienced. You'll see a mere foreign graduate managing people with decades of experience and qualification. It's downright insulting. My own prayer is that it's a woman this time, or a man of integrity so nobody will be making my work difficult."

Simon chuckled. "And what if she turns out to be a lesbian?"

"Ha!" I snap my fingers. "God forbid. It will never happen. So that's your plan for me, boy?"

My hand landed on his shoulder in a playful slap as he slowed down beside my house gate.

"I am not a boy, Glory."

"Thank you very much, Mr. Man. Goodnight," I said as I alighted and knocked on my gate.

As usual, he stayed behind until Musa, my gate man, had opened my gate and I entered the compound before driving off.

CHAPTER TWO

My parents were already asleep. Jaja, my kid brother, was watching MTV in the parlour. I grimaced at the sight of half-naked girls, flashy cars, and diamonds making up the music of today. Jaja. With his youthful zeal, he could easily be led down the wrong path.

I said a short prayer for him as I retired for the night, gazing up to my star-filled ceiling while on my back on my bed. I had filled the ceiling with glow-in-the-dark star stickers, arranging them like a comet. My room was my one vanity. I didn't spare any expense. With my salary, I had repainted the walls bright pink and deep purple, different from the creamy white colour of the rest of the house, and had livened it up with colourful vases and throw pillows. I'd even hung a fancy curtain beside my bed.

But tonight, all of this didn't make me relax. I tossed and turned 'til morning, spending the entire Saturday cleaning up the whole house and rehearsing the Tyson Pierce song until I had perfected the alto part. I would not be cleaning the entire house myself, if not for the fact that Nene, the cousin who lived with us, had not returned home in three days now. My mother said she has gone back to the village, spreading vicious rumours about her. I have tried so often to intercede in their quarrels, but they are both strong-headed and opinionated women.

My mother has accused me several times of being too short-sighted, of not seeing Nene for the wicked and malicious person she is. But then, she sees a lot of people from her husband's family as wicked and out to get her.

16

Maybe the fact most of my father's family were openly and heatedly against their marriage had helped to sour any relationships they might have had.

Once, when my mother had had only me for ten years, they had supposedly brought another woman for my father as a wife. "This one will bring you sons."

My father had sent them and the new wife packing immediately, and for a while, things had been tense.

I still remember her tears, and later, whoops of joy when she took in again and finally had Jaja. As a previous only child, I had welcomed the interruption and the company. I didn't mind it that most, if not all, of my parents' attentions were on the new, squalling baby, the man of the house.

Now, I have gotten used to his status, how His Royal Manliness is not supposed to do any menial house chores except wash the car, and then, not even my car. No. I had to bribe him to wash my car.

But I love Jaja with all my heart, his nerdy glasses, and his ability to burst into laughter at every opportune time. His humour had eased my mother's attitude greatly, she who was known as 'The Worrier.'

She worries about everything imaginable, and I sometimes yell at her, "You are not God. You can't control everything."

Her worry did not let me attend the Lagos excursion trip my secondary school classmates had gone to. Her worry did not let me stay on campus during my university days, and her worry had refused to let me move into my own place.

"*Tufiakwa*," she had muttered when I'd suggested it. "You will only leave this house to your husband's house."

Bringing Nene, my cousin, into the house had been a breeze. My father, in a typical manly attitude, had suddenly announced she would be staying with us as he would put her through school.

I remember my mother's tightly squeezed face as she'd muttered, "Before you will say I don't like your relatives again ..." to which my father had said, "There she goes again!", honestly baffled.

I love my father and all, but he is not the best man to notice details. He barely knows what's going on. A professor in the state university, his nose is always inside textbooks with high-sounding words. He doesn't have the time to notice the sneer on his elder sisters' face, or a slight one of his relatives may have done. Heck, half the time, he forgets where he keeps his keys, his socks, and is generally scatter-brained.

Good thing my mother is meticulous, all about the details. She sees and knows all. When I was little, I used to imagine she had eyes in the back of her head. How else would she know when I was rolling my eyes at her behind her back when she was yelling at me to get my chores done, or that I hadn't dusted the back of the television?

For a while, I had waited for her to lose her braids and wretchedly pulled her hair apart while she slept, hoping to see two eyes behind her head. All I got was a slap and a yelling.

But most of the time, my mother is right. I, too, had noticed how my father's sisters sometimes sneered at her, the turning down of their nose and all. Being a confrontational person, my mom laughed out-rightly in their face as they all pretended to get along for the sake of my father.

I don't have anything against her, Nene, the girl whose presence helped in the house. I could now go to bed without washing the plates at night as Jaja's hands are too manly for such work like washing plates, cleaning, or cooking. I don't have to rush from office straight into the kitchen as my mother says she is preparing me for the rigors of married life.

Her presence had eased the work, and even though she maintained a strained relationship with my mother, we were on cordial terms.

Rehearsals that Saturday were a breeze, and soon, Sunday dawned bright and clear. Even the birds were chirping and the trees swayed to the cold wind making swirling noises, the sun hiding behind clouds. It was one of those mornings with a promise of rain. I went to my car and removed my umbrella before waiting for Simon at the gate. My parents and Jaja attend a different church.

I started attending my church during my university years, and clearly remember the struggles and fights I'd had to go through to get my parents to accept the fact I wouldn't be a member of the family church anymore. Their church is okay, but they don't have a vibrant youth culture. The service is usually long and monotonous, and I never could develop any real relationship with the elderly members. The few people around my age who did attend all had elderly mannerisms and tendencies. Imagine my relief when Chioma, a school mate at the time, invited me for an evening service, and for the first time, church was fun, educating, and still very religious. All I can say is the fight was worth it. I had said the salvation creed back in secondary school, and I hadn't meant it then, but my church had brought me so much closer to God, I could never give that up now.

My parents still view my church with suspicion, especially during night vigils where popular gospel music artists are invited. They don't understand why we have to spend hours rehearsing, or why I must attend all the weekly activities, or, the one time they attended my church, why everybody is so young and loud.

Simon arrived right on time and picked me up in front of my gate. As choir members, we were required to be in church by seven a.m. for prayers before service began.

It seemed like a normal Sunday service, except, it wasn't. I didn't expect anything out of the norm. I was in the choir unit beside the pulpit, patting down my skirt, when Pastor Lanre entered with his guest.

They took the seats in front as the opening prayer was being made. I couldn't close my eyes. My heart was racing. Was it him? It couldn't possibly be. I hadn't seen him in such a long time. How could it be? Still, I looked again, pinching myself to be certain I wasn't dreaming. I kept looking at the young man sitting beside Pastor Lanre, not quite believing my eyes.

"Chioma, do you know the person Pastor invited today?"

Chioma looked at me strangely. "So you don't know him. That's Pastor Lanre's first son."

"What? Are you for real?"

"Yes. He's the one who was schooling abroad."

"Okay. What is his name?"

Maybe it wasn't him, just somebody who looked exactly like him. I must be wrong.

When Chioma said his name, I knew. It was him.

But how did he become Pastor Lanre's son? Oh! He'd told me his father was a pastor back then. Never did I imagine my pastor would be his father.

At that moment, he turned to look directly at me. I tried to smile. It didn't work. A hard look entered his eyes, and he glanced away, his jaw hardening like he was gritting his teeth. Didn't he recognise me? And why did he look away like he was angry at me?

Okay, you don't know who the guy is, right?

God! How do I explain?

I have to start at the very beginning, and we have to go way back when...

PART TWO
Genesis

CHAPTER THREE

Do you know what it's like to have a crush on somebody who doesn't even know you exist?

So there he is, laughing with his friends, talking to girls from his class and girls not from his class. From my vantage point, peeping outside my classroom window, I'm staring and wondering what these girls have that I don't. What makes them so special, anyways?

Oh, sure, they are the beautiful and confident girls who find it easy to be friends with boys, and most importantly, they are extremely confident—they seem to know themselves and carry these mature personae I have never been able to achieve. These girls always appear perfect, hair expertly put in place, uniform ironed and clean always, no stains or spills, not even ice cream spills. Their socks are always sparkling white even after school.

I, on the other hand, have socks so black and dirty, sometimes I wonder if it's from the dust or if everybody lines up after class to step on my feet every day. I have no senior friend who could help me iron. When I do have ice cream, it's like a tornado of stains on my uniform, forming a map from here to the whole of Africa.

And most importantly, I don't talk to boys. It's not a hype thing or a classy thing. But somewhere between Jss2 and Jss3, I stopped talking to boys entirely. None, not one. Which is weird, considering I go to a mixed school.

And I have these awesome conversations with them in my head. I'm funny and would be great friends with boys, but the shyness and the persona of the dark, quiet, angry girl who never smiles is a tough shell to break. Maybe at first, they noticed me, but now, I've faded into the wood work. Like a wallflower—glanced at, used as a prop to lean on, but never seen, never noticed.

It's not like I don't smile. It's just, every time a boy comes close, a hard frown appears automatically to hide the fact I'm nervous. So all I do is have crushes on cute guys and wonder how girls start up friendships with boys. And what do they even talk about?

That's the big question. I always imagine the conversation to be an intelligent, great one. When the boys look at me, there is this blank expression in their face, like I am just one of the many other people who occupy space and have no meaning.

But they pay so much special attention to the pretty girls. The kind of pretty girls that are popular. I used to think I was pretty, too. At home, everyone used to compliment me and tell me how tall, slim, and beautiful I was. I believed it.

Until I came to school ... and discovered there is pretty, *then* there is pretty.

Maybe my kind of pretty needs deliberate and exaggerated lighting. But these girls didn't need any of that. Their pretty was obvious.

They date the most popular and the finest boys in our class. Something which amazes me is why the Obviously Handsome boys—it's what I call the people who are pretty and everybody knows it. Not me. I am pretty and nobody knows it—would somehow always date the Obviously Pretty girls.

It always galled and fascinated me. Like, do they call a secret meeting for the handsome boys and pretty girls the rest of us, the Ordinaries, are not aware of? Is it not the same class we all attend? Yet, tomorrow, I'll see one Pretty girl, laughing with and dating another Handsome boy, and I'll be wondering, when did all this start? Where are these meetings I never get invited to?

But enough of that.

I am still at my window, where I am peeping at a boy I like who is talking to one beautiful girl. It hurts me a lot. Who is she? Just because I'm too quiet and shy to talk to boys does not mean I'm not fun to talk to. It's just because I'm not so beautiful. So I remove my head from the window and sit down.

I remember one day, I was walking home from class, tired, hungry, and angry at my parents for not sending me money the previous weekend.

You see, the thing about public boarding school is, once your money and provisions are finished, then you're entirely at the mercy of the school dining. And God save you if you don't have a plate.

I was in that boat—money gone, provisions gone, and no friend to lean on. I was walking back to the dorm after a tiring day of classes I'd hardly paid any attention to, my head down, my mind far away, when I heard the sound of a voice that made me look up.

There, at the four-point junction leading to the dining hall, the girls' dorm, and staff quarters, stood Alex, along with other male friends, laughing. Normally, as junior students, they would never dare stand at the junction, but the senior students were writing their Mock exams in the dining hall, giving us some few hours of freedom. Of course, being in Jss3 didn't mean much freedom, especially if somebody in a senior class came along. But nobody else was around, and Alex and his friends were taking advantage of this few precious minutes of rare freedom.

But my mind barely registered all that. My heart had started beating fast again, and my legs had stopped moving. The sudden urge to turn back and go the other way tugged at me. *Why are you running?* I asked myself. *What's the point? It's not like Alex knows you exist or anything.* So what was the point of all this hide and seek? No point at all.

I would pass there, and they wouldn't even bother to look at me, talk of acknowledging me.

But it didn't matter much. Even though they didn't know I existed, I knew they did. Especially Alex. Oh, how I knew Alex existed. Sometimes, in my dark, bleary world, the only spot of sunshine would be the times I would catch a glimpse of him in class or in the dining hall. Which wasn't often.

You see, though we were all in Jss3, Alex and I were not in the same class. He was in D class, I was in B class, which meant we learnt in different classrooms. So I only saw Alex in brief moments when he walked down the classroom corridors past my class and I would be peeping through the window. I had made the habit of always watching the corridor like a hawk. Sometimes, I think that's the main reason I chose a seat by the window.

Other times, when I ventured outside my class and walked past his, I would see him inside, never alone, always surrounded by friends. And girls, Pretty girls. Especially that Miriam girl. Maybe it was the fact Alex was tall, dark-skinned, and had a bit of muscle. Or because by far, he was the neatest boy in Jss3 with his sparkling white shirts that were always ironed. Or maybe because he was also intelligent. Me, I was an average student, not at the bottom of my class, but not at the top, either.

Other times, I would catch glimpses of Alex in the dining hall. But this wasn't often. He wasn't a 'grubber' as we called those always too eager for dining hall food. And even when I would see him, he would always be in the company of senior boys.

So, you see, Alex was a special, special boy. Sure, he didn't know I existed, but I sure did. I noticed everything, from the small cut he had on the back of his neck from a bad haircut, to his clean-cut fingernails. Sometimes, I would imagine those hands around my shoulders, his face bent close to mine as he talked to me in whispers.

But all that was non-essential because there stood Alex in front of me. And I had been standing and staring for a few minutes now. I couldn't do it. I couldn't walk past them. I would surely miss my step, or slip and fall, or walk awkwardly. No matter what, I didn't want Alex to see me.

Just as I made up my mind to turn back and wait in the parking lot of the Admin block until the coast was clear, Alex suddenly turned sideways, straight towards me.

Oh, no! He had seen me. What would I do? I couldn't possibly turn and go back now. It would be too obvious I was too chicken to walk past them. Neither could I walk past them. I was too chicken to do that!

So I stood there, then had a flash of inspiration. Turning my head away, I removed my bag, opened it, and brought out a notebook, then nodded slowly like I had just remembered something. I closed the bag, still holding the book, and turned back quickly, like one in a great hurry, and walked away.

I don't know how convincing I was, but anything was better than nothing. And I had avoided another disaster. I stood in the parking lot for a good thirty minutes, before I could build up the courage to check if they had left.

The coast was clear. I smiled benignly as I walked past the previously dangerous spot. Of course, the thirty minutes

I had wasted meant the senior students had finished their exams, and the moment I entered the dorm room, we were forced to take a siesta. I couldn't wash like I had planned to. But it was worth it. I think so. Wasn't it?

***

One new term, I had a goal—to not be the quiet and depressed wallflower of a girl anymore. I was tired of watching others laugh and live life to the fullest. I was tired of observing others being happy. I wanted to be happy myself.

So during the long break after we had written our Junior WAEC exams, I made a resolution to be a changed person. I had a plan—to make more female friends, and most importantly, some male friends. And possibly, quite possibly, maybe by a stroke of luck or miracle, I would find a way to talk to Alex. It wouldn't necessarily be a relationship thing, but at least, we could be casual acquaintances. And if all went well, from there, we could be friends, and who knew where it may lead to.

But come what may, Alex or no Alex, I would most definitely strive to be happy this new term.

My mother took me to the market to buy blue check material to sew my dormitory day wear. I was in Charity House, and Charity House wore blue day wears. I insisted on going with her to the tailor just so I could insist she wouldn't make my skirts too long.

All through my Junior classes, my mother had always insisted on extra-long tunics for me. They had been a constant source of embarrassment for me. I mean, other girls wore tunics just slightly below their knee. But my mother insisted on making mine so long they almost reached my ankle.

By sheer force of will, I convinced the tailor to keep my skirt just slightly below my knee. She agreed, much to my mother's dismay.

The plan was good and ready to go. 'Til I entered the school compound. The first person I saw was Miriam.

You see, we were now in SS1, which means we would now wear skirts. No more tunics. And we had all been anticipating this for a while. So when I saw Miriam, in a beautiful skirt falling just above her knee, her beautiful face glowing with life and happiness, I immediately took the form of the opposite: Dark, angry, unhappy, and sad.

How could I hope to be as beautiful and happy as her? I was the sole meaning of darkness. Sometimes, I don't fade into the wall—I am literarily the wall. Nobody cares or notices me.

And I stood there with my box, watching other girls greet their friends affectionately and laughing gaily. I had no friend. Not one. No one came to meet me gaily. I picked up my box, hung my bucket on my elbow, and entered the dormitory.

I could hear talks of calls and visits during the holiday. I hadn't received any call or visit during the holidays nor made any, having no one to call or visit.

But my anger was not about all that. No! My anger came from the fact that almost all the SS1 girls came with skirts falling just above their knees. Three inches above their knees, to be precise. I soon found out we had a new senior boarding house mistress, and she had told them just before the long break she didn't like long skirts and gave them permission to sew skirts three inches above their knees when coming back.

I hadn't known about a new senior boarding house mistress, or about the skirt thing. And no one had told me.

Of course, I hadn't asked. And who would I ask? Most of the girls in the dormitory didn't know I was alive, especially my classmates. The few times I'd ventured to ask some of them some questions, the look on their face had been one of utter contempt. One of the disadvantages of not having friends, especially friends from your class, was not having access to some vital information you'd missed somehow. Like how everyone except me knew the biology teacher was going to give a test, and now, how everyone knew about the skirt thing, except me.

***

Yeah, I was a senior student, and I had automatic rights to send the junior students on any errand, but I never did. I was too afraid. Too afraid they wouldn't respect me, obey me, or even listen to me. The junior students would most definitely see me as nothing, too, just as everyone else did.

So I ran all my errands myself. While other SS1 girls would send the junior girls to fetch their buckets, sweep their corners and all that, I did it all myself. And whenever I would see a junior student watching me as I carried my bucket or swept my corner, I would pretend I didn't feel ashamed or humiliated. I would tell myself I was only being kind to them, that I didn't like sending my juniors on errands.

However, I always sensed they knew I was afraid of them. I mean, the fear had to be written all over me. Just one more deep wound on my body.

Though I planned to make friends, it wasn't easy. Every time I tried to talk to somebody, anybody, I would get too scared and leave. The only person I talked to was my seat mate Hadiza, just to ask her to borrow a pen or pencil or such stuff. Hadiza had her own set of friends, and she only sat on our seat when a teacher was in class. I think she chose that seat just because it was the only available one.

But, something wonderful happened to me in the middle of term, just before we wrote our second tests. I became friends with someone a lot higher in the social ladder than I had ever imagined.

CHAPTER FOUR

That day, I was going down to the shop beside the dining hall to buy chewing gum for Nene, a senior girl in my house.

It was just after we had eaten egusi soup and eba in the dining, and the sun was really fierce that afternoon. As I was walking back to the dining, I was angry, grumbling at going back there just minutes after leaving it, all just to buy gum. I got to the shop and asked the woman to bring me chewing gum. She put it in a black polythene bag and gave it to me. Then, someone behind me asked me gently, "All this gum, just for you?"

I turned back. I didn't know the boy, but he was most definitely an SS3 boy—he had a Peace House check over a Charity House check. No junior student could ever try that. You see, we were required to only wear our house colours, but the SS3 students, especially the boys, sometimes interchanged these colours. You could see them wearing a Charity House shirt over a Peace House trouser.

Somehow, I smiled back at him as he looked at the amount of chewing gum in my bag, which was ridiculous. Senior Nene was known for chewing gum loudly in the dormitory.

"Is it for you?" he asked me.

I shook my head.

"Who sent you?" he then asked.

"Senior Nene," I replied.

He laughed at this. "So Nene sent you to buy all this gum. After asking junior girls to smuggle egusi soup for her, she wants to use the gum to eat the egusi, abi?"

In the boarding house, it was forbidden to take food out of the dining hall. And most senior students, especially the girls, didn't usually come to the dining. They were too big to come and eat eba and soup in full view of their male classmates. So they would ask us to smuggle food out of the dining hall for them.

Of course, this meant coming up with ingenious ways. Sometimes, some girls would even put the food in their school bag just to sneak it out. But this was only when a teacher was around. Most times, when it was just us students, we would get the food and simply hold it in our hands.

The SS3 boy was still laughing, and somehow, I laughed, too. And that's how I made my first friend. His name was ... okay, I can't really recall his name, but his nickname was NFA, short for No Future Ambition. Looking back now, I realize what a horrible nickname it was. But NFA became my friend. He would call me whenever he saw me, and we would talk. Mostly, he would ask me questions, and I would reply.

Then one day, while we were sitting in my classroom block, he asked me the *big* question. "Who's your boyfriend?"

I laughed. I laughed so hard, I think he got confused. He got the idea.

"How can you not have a boyfriend, a fine girl like you?"

He seemed genuinely confused, and I looked at him in surprise. I mean, couldn't he see I was not beautiful, or bold, or anything? Couldn't he notice I didn't even have a single friend? Or that nobody spoke to me?

But I could tell he was genuinely surprised. So here I was, with a boy who honestly thought I was a beautiful girl with lots of friends and a boyfriend. I became ashamed, ashamed to tell him I was a nobody.

So I shrugged, like it didn't mean much, like being boyfriend-less was all my idea. He looked at me speculatively, like it was too hard to believe. I felt good, good that somebody could actually believe I had a life. I smiled all day.

But before he left that day, he said, "I will send somebody to you."

I guess he meant he would send a boy to me, someone to be my boyfriend.

I would like to say it all ended happily, that his friendship caused me to open up, I made some friends, eventually had a boyfriend, etc. But nothing happened.

He graduated. And that was it. My only friend graduated. And secretly, I kept hoping and looking for the boy he would send to me. But nobody came.

***

I decided to start making my hair in my SS1 second term. I had been on a low cut since my Jss1 at my mother's insistence. She seemed to think making my hair will somehow distract me from my studies. Now, almost every girl who had been on a low cut had saved their hair during the long break and was now plaiting it. So I began saving mine.

After about three weeks, I met a girl called Adanma to plait it for me. Adanma had always been very kind to me, and she agreed. But when we started to comb out my afro, she discovered the hair was still too short for her to plait it properly, but I insisted.

So began the most painful experience of my life. I have never experienced pain like that, coupled with the fact Adanma was just an amateur in plaiting hair. To date, the left upper section of my head is sore. I still wince whenever someone plaits that part of my hair.

After Adanma had finished with the hair, it looked okay, manageable for very, very short hair. But by Tuesday, the hair had begun to pull out of the edges, making me look like I hadn't combed it properly. I couldn't comb it out because I didn't have the time to make it again until the weekend.

Soon, a classmate said my hair looked like somebody threw up on my head. It didn't really affect me. Until the day I almost ran into Alex. I was so self-conscious about the hair, as usual, I ran into hiding. That week, I became 007, the way I would scout the area just to make sure Alex was nowhere in sight, and if I sighted him afar, I would most definitely throw cartwheels just to make sure he didn't see me.

You have to understand it wasn't the fear of talking to Alex that made me run this time. It was my hair. No matter how shy I was, I had made up my mind to talk to him before the term ended. I just didn't want anything to spoil the moment.

I could only breathe easily when the week ended, and I continued saving my afro, pressing down hard on it to make it look like a low cut.

***

Something happened to me that term. I became friends with a new student in my house, a fat black girl named Adeola. I had lost my bucket, so she began sharing hers with me. We would bathe together with the bucket, then fetch it and keep it under her bed. Adeola was a very outgoing person. And a bully. She used her weight to bully our classmates out of their monies, provisions, food, or even plates when she didn't have any. For the first time, I had a protector, someone to walk with to class, someone to talk to during the evening prep.

One evening, during the games period, I made another friend. The games period was held during a chosen afternoon when, instead of our nap, we would wear white shorts and shirts and go to the school field to practice our match parade, long jump, high jump, shot put, and whatever else kind of sport was available.

That evening, I left the field early and went back to the dormitory so I could dress up for the evening food before everyone else. You see, the game period was also a time SS3 students used to deal heavily with the junior students. While we would be out there in the field, enjoying ourselves, they would lie in wait for us from the dormitory gate to the rooms, barely giving us time to wash our legs, change to our day wear, grab our plates, and run to the dining. And God help you if you didn't have your complete items that day.

So to avoid all this, I had left the field early enough, had my bath, and was fetching water when I met Pelumi at the tap. She had also left the field early to prepare for the evening food. Somehow, we got talking, and that evening, we walked to the dining hall together. People were looking at us like we had grown horns. And maybe we had.

What you should understand is how Pelumi was the crème de la crème of our set, part of the clique of beautiful and popular girls. Pelumi was also a very neat girl, her socks and shirts always sparkling white. Of course, it helped she was friends with a lot of SS3 girls, something I had never managed to achieve.

So when I became friends with her, I couldn't really believe it. And from that evening, Pelumi drew me close. We would walk to class together, spend time talking and laughing in her dorm room. She even began to introduce me to her friends, and they also started to become my friends.

Of course, I also had to change some things about me so I could fit in to their group. I began to take very, very good care of my appearance, brush my hair neatly, bleach all my shirts, do my possible best to iron, and make sure nobody stepped on me so my socks would remain clean all day. Pelumi was very careful about these things. Every time I came to her, she would look at me from head to toe and assess me, telling me where I had gone wrong and where I got it right.

I must admit, I am still grateful to her 'til today. Prior to meeting her, I hadn't really cared about my appearance, but she opened my eyes, so to speak. Somehow, I couldn't believe I was slowly but surely becoming a member of the clique of beautiful and popular girls. As usual, something happened to spoil it all for me.

One day, Pelumi called me aside and began advising me to stop being friends with Adeola because Adeola had a body odour. You see, I knew the main problem was that Adeola didn't fit into their group; she was too carefree and non-pretentious. And since I was becoming a member of their clique, I couldn't hang around just anybody anymore. I had to make sure I only hung out with the popular and pretty girls to maintain their image.

Even though she didn't come out to say it like that, I began to mull it over in my mind. How could I stop being friends with Adeola, someone who had been my only friend for a long time before Pelumi deigned to even look at me? Adeola, the girl whose body odour probably came from the fact she had to share her bucket with me.

I still don't know how I found the strength to say no to Pelumi. Pelumi had become like a surrogate mother to me—I valued her opinion and friendship so much. I did whatever she told me to do. But there was no way I could betray Adeola, the only real friend I had. I started avoiding Pelumi until gradually, our friendship diminished to nothing.

It didn't help that Adeola left school the next term after she found out she was to repeat a class. I went back to not having a real friend, but whenever I look back, I am glad I hadn't betrayed Adeola. Truly.

Soon after this, the rumour began to spread that Alex was now officially dating Miriam. Yeah, my heart broke literally into a thousand pieces. I did cry, but only at night when nobody could see me. I felt betrayed, but I knew I couldn't blame anybody, not even me. How could someone like Alex date someone like me? It was impossible, but my heart had held on to foolish hope.

Then, two weeks later, another nasty rumour began to spread about Alex. Apparently, Alex had only asked Miriam out on a dare, and now that he had won the bet, he had dumped her.

Listen, I am not a vindictive person; I don't find joy in other people's sorrow, but boy, I was so glad, so relieved. But still, what Alex had done was cruel, and even though I was excited he was still unattached, I wasn't happy with what he had done.

Miriam cried her eyes out in the dormitory, and even though she wasn't my friend, I sympathised with her.

One cool evening, I wasn't feeling too well, so I walked down to the sick bay to get some drugs. Alex was there, lying on the bed receiving drip. At first, the shyness wanted to overwhelm me, but then, somehow, I held my ground. It didn't matter so much anymore. For three years, I had been harbouring a crush, an infatuation for someone who didn't even know I exist, someone who had cruelly dumped another girl.

What did it matter, anyway? It was obvious he didn't like me. Maybe because I wasn't so beautiful, but I like myself. I like how I look, and if it wasn't enough for him, then he didn't deserve me. Someday, I would leave this school and meet a nice, handsome guy who would love me back.

All these ran through my mind as I swallowed my pills, totally ignoring the sleeping Alex on the bed beside me. But then, just as I was about to leave, he said something, something that made me turn. He called my name.

CHAPTER FIVE

Very slowly, I turned. My heart was already beating very fast—I felt like I was in a marathon while my heart was screaming, *'He knows my name, he knows my name, he knows my name!'*

Oh, well, when I did turn, Alex was still sleeping. It was just my imagination.

Before you get angry, let me tell you how, at this point, my life started changing.

I think I began to feel emboldened from Adeola and Pelumi's friendship. The people I thought were all high and mighty suddenly became just ordinary human beings to me.

I just couldn't see them as before. And with this new insight, my life began to change slowly. I wasn't so anxious and shy anymore. I began to talk to people, in my class, my dorm room, even began to send the junior students.

Let me tell you something that helped. One day, we SS1 girls had been sent to mop the entire girls' dorm as a punishment. So I finished early and went downstairs to the tap to take a bath. Somehow, as I climbed the staircase and got to the base, I heard my name coming from the junior dorm. Curious, I tiptoed to the door to overhear the conversation. I couldn't see the faces, but I knew it was three junior girls discussing.

One was saying, "But that senior Glory is too quiet. She doesn't even talk to anybody."

"Yes, but me, I like her, sha. She doesn't really like sending us. And she's not wicked. Do you know one day, she helped me to fetch water at the tap?" the other one replied.

"Yes, me, too. She has given me her plate to use before, one day when I didn't have any plate," the third girl replied.

It was the best conversation I ever overheard. Maybe I had been wrong about myself all along. I wasn't as bad as I thought. People liked me, even as quiet and as shy as I was. I think the problem was I didn't like myself, too busy comparing myself to others to fully appreciate me for me.

But the truth is, I am not a quiet person, not at all. In all my life until now, I'd always been talkative. It's just that when I came I this school, I stopped smiling and talking. I think it's because my best friend Ebele died two weeks before I came to this school.

You see, Ebele and I had been best friends since nursery school. We used to do everything together. Sometimes during the holiday, I would spend some weeks in her house, and she would come to mine the rest of the holiday. They say she died of malaria. We had planned to come to this school together. We both passed the entrance exam and gained admission together.

I guess her death affected me a lot. Funny enough, I hadn't thought of her in a while. I just carried her like a burden around my shoulders.

Anyways, I was walking down the classroom block to get to my Form teacher's office when, as usual, I looked into Alex's class, just to catch a glimpse of him as I passed. I think the fates where working for me because, somehow, just as I looked into the class, Alex was also looking out the window.

So yeah, our eyes met, and for one brief moment, I stood there, not panicking, just looking at him as he looked at me … before I remembered I was standing outside a window peeping at a boy. Embarrassed would be an understatement, and despite my dark skin, I think anyone looking could see the blood rise to my face. I glanced away and walked out with hurried steps.

But it was impossible to get it off my mind. I think that day was the very first time Alex looked at me. I was feeling tingly with excitement and apprehension. Even though I hadn't actually talked to him, I felt happy that, at least, he knew I existed. I wasn't so much of an invisible wallflower anymore.

The next morning, Alex was standing by the window beside the door of my class. As usual, my legs forgot how to walk, and I almost tripped, concentrating so hard on not falling, I forgot to frown. And as I passed by him, I could swear he smiled at me, like, really smiled at me. I responded with a frown.

But my heart melted. Oh, to have his beautiful face smiling at me, just me. That evening, I had a lot of class notes to copy, so I stayed back in class after school to copy them.

Soon, the classroom block was empty and quiet. If I could complete the notes before going to the dorm that evening, I would have time to finish the book I was reading that night. But it started to feel like somebody was watching me. I turned and looked around. Nobody was there. Just as I finished and started preparing to leave, I heard footsteps walking away and looked up just in time to see somebody walk past my class.

I couldn't be sure, but I think it was Alex. Had he been watching me all this while? And for what? Maybe it wasn't even him, just my imagination running wild. Why would Alex be peering at me from a window? And what would he even be doing here after class hours?

The sheer audacity of it made me smile at my own antics. Whether it was foolishness or hope, I have no idea. But then, something magical happened during the last week of school before Christmas break.

You see, a new female principal had been transferred to our school that term. And she came with radical ideas. She was appalled how though it was a mixed school, the two sexes were still not comfortable in each other's presence.

She made a lot of sense to me. I mean, why should I still be shy being around boys when I go to a mixed school? So the new principal began to change some things. First, she forced boys and girls in the same houses to sit together in the dining. I don't even want to talk about how mortifying and embarrassing it was at first. Do you know what it takes to eat your food comfortably sitting right in front of boys? But after a while, we got used to it.

Secondly, she introduced 'Social Night.' Prior to the new principal coming, my school didn't have anything like social activities organised. We just went about our businesses. But that term, the last evening before the term closed, the first Social Night was organised. We had to stay behind after the evening food to arrange the hall for the event. Then, we rushed back to the dorm to prepare.

The senior girls came out decked in the shortest skirts they could find, their faces painted, lips shining and pouting.

We couldn't do any of that. So we looked deep inside our bags for our shorter skirts and lip glosses. There was so much excitement that evening, so many borrowing of skirts and lip gloss and hair ribbons, etc. When we finally got the hall, we looked our very best.

The hall was full, and music was playing from the speakers set up all around. The dining tables had been taken away, the chairs arranged in squares to create a wide space in the middle of the hall for dancing.

At first, there was a lot of shyness, but after the first few bold people went to the dance floor, the shyness disappeared.

I didn't know how to dance, and no way would I embarrass myself on the dance floor. So I sat down and watched the dancers.

I knew the moment Alex entered the hall. The truth is, I had been watching out for him. Somehow, I was scared because I didn't want him dancing with any girl. It would just break my heart. But that was impossible—Alex was popular, and somehow, he *would* find his way to the dance floor. I watched surreptitiously as he stood with his friends looking at the dancers. His friends began to disappear one by one, each with a girl on the dance floor, 'til he was left standing alone. It wouldn't be long now. Very soon, he would go dance with somebody. I couldn't watch this. I looked down at the floor, not wanting to see anything that would break my heart.

When I looked up, Alex wasn't there anymore. Even though I told myself I was being silly, I still looked for him at the dance floor. He wasn't there, either. Maybe he had left. Or he was outside with somebody else.

Feeling bereft, I stood up and left the hall to stand by the window outside, just wishing for the night to be over so I could go to sleep. But when I looked across to the next window, Alex was there, and he was looking at me. He was alone.

I bowed my head and looked into the hall, pretending to be busy. But I could feel his eyes on me. Excitement and apprehension made me giddy. Finally, maybe he was beginning to see me, to notice me. I summoned up the courage to look back at him. He smiled. I smiled back a little. Then, he left the window and walked until he was standing next to me.

At this point, I felt like we were the only two people in the world. He was so close, I could see the small sheen of sweat on his neck, the small scratch on his wristwatch. He kept coming closer, and I kept shrinking into the wall. When he held my hand, it was like I was exploding into a thousand happy pieces. My body began to tingle; I couldn't keep still. With his other hand, he held my chin and raised my face up to meet his.

Then, the lights went off. And he kissed me.

CHAPTER SIX

I melted! I couldn't think straight. His lips were soft, softer than I had imagined. I didn't want him to stop. He pulled me closer, his hand on my waist and the other on my hair. I had never felt anything like this.

Instinctively, I hugged him tighter and kissed him back with every passion, every love I had felt for him all these years. It wasn't enough. He pushed me back gently 'til my back touched the wall, then continued his assault on my lips—soft, light feathery kisses that had me falling against him. If he hadn't been holding me, I would have fallen.

When the lights came back on, my sanity returned. How could I have just let him kiss me like this? He hadn't even said a word to me. Was I so easy and cheap? And what if it was another bet? What if he was playing a cruel joke on me like he had done with Miriam?

Suddenly, I felt like throwing up. I pushed his hand away and ran out with the crowd of girls leaving the hall. I ran until I got the dorm and lay in my bed, feeling ashamed. While one part of me was happy Alex had kissed me, the rational part was calling me stupid. Stupid to let a boy I'd never talked to, a boy who had rudely dumped another girl on a bet, to kiss me.

But, oh, he kissed so well. I couldn't get it out of my mind. And I wanted more. My lips felt soft and yielding. I tossed and turned all through the night in confusion. The next morning, I decided I would go talk to him and get some answers before we took our results and went home for the holiday.

But when I got to classroom block, the first person I saw was Alex standing outside his classroom door talking to Miriam. He didn't even notice me watching them. They laughed together, then he held her hand, and they both entered their classroom.

***

I travelled to my village that Christmas and ate so much, I put on weight. My mom was happy. She had always said I was too skinny.

I began to do more house chores, went to church with her regularly, all just to persuade her to change my school, but she was adamant. Nothing I said could change her mind. I even told her the male teachers sometimes molested the female students—she didn't believe me.

To be truthful, I wasn't lying. I had almost been molested by a male teacher once before. Mr. Collins, my Maths teacher, had called me to his office once when I was in Jss2 and had shown me how poorly I was doing in my result, promising to change my grade to a better one. He'd then asked me if I was a neat girl. I said yes. He said I had to prove it by showing him my thighs, because neat girls had light-complexioned thighs. I foolishly and innocently raised my tunic up for him to see my lap. I don't know why he hadn't gone further that day. I think God had just wanted to save me the trauma.

But I couldn't tell my mother all that. So I cooked up stories, none of which she believed. So yeah, I did go back to school, but I made up my mind never to even look at any boy again.

The first week, I didn't see him. I hated him so much, I refused to call his name, even in my mind. So when I did see him the second week, walking to the classroom block, I ran inside my class and pretended my heart wasn't breaking. Oh, I hated him. His face; the very sight of him. I had been praying that somehow, by a miracle, he wouldn't return.

At the end of class, as I carried my bag, I saw him, standing outside my class window and looking at me, smiling. I glared angrily at him. He frowned slightly. I hissed and went outside.

"Hi ..." he called out to me.

I raised my head up and walked past him like he was air. Let him go and talk to Miriam, to all the other girls in this school—I didn't care. At all. But he shouldn't pretend like he knew me or even liked me. Maybe he had come to mock me, to prove to his friends he really had kissed me and probably won the bet. I wondered how much he'd won this time.

Tears fell down my eyes, and I angrily swiped them. I would not cry for any cheap human being hopping from one girl to the other, kissing one girl today and another the next. Just my luck I fell in love with a cheat, a big womaniser.

It served me right. But I wouldn't shed another tear for that one. During the evening dining, for the first time, he came to my table and sat down right in front of me. I ignored my beating heart and concentrated on my food.

"Why are you avoiding me?" he asked me.

I ignored him and put a spoon of rice in my mouth, chewing slowing. The other boys at the table looked at us strangely. Mabel, the girl sitting next to me, looked puzzled.

"I'm talking to you. Why are you avoiding me? Now I'm here to talk, and you're ignoring me. What's wrong with you?"

He was starting to get angry.

And I was angry, too. How dare he imply something was wrong with me when he was the world's biggest cheat and liar? I had had enough.

"It's you that something is wrong with, not me!" I shouted at him.

Heads turned to look at us.

He glared at me angrily, then stood up and walked away. I went back to my food with so much concentration, ignoring the stunned silence at the table.

"Why did you shout at him like that? I didn't even know you guys were friends," Mabel said to me.

I smiled and said nothing. She was the school's big gossip.

"Ha, okay, oh! All these quiet and deadly people," Mabel said and went back to her food, looking at me occasionally in confusion.

That evening, many girls came to ask me about the dining hall incident. I lied and said he had misplaced my notebook. I didn't look at them when they questioned what a science student would be looking for in an art student's notebook. Let them think whatever they wanted to. I knew some of them were envious. I wished I could transfer my pain to them. They could all have him if they wanted. I didn't care anymore.

When Alex saw me the next day, he frowned and looked away. I frowned, too, and walked past. Maybe it just wasn't meant to be. And so we went on, frowning and looking away when we saw each other.

That term, I refused to sit by the window. I didn't want to keep seeing Alex pass by or talk to other girls. So I exchanged my seat with Michael who sat in the middle row—I think he likes Hadiza, my seat mate—and sat with Chika, Michael's former seat mate.

Chika was an intelligent boy, the most brilliant one in my class. But he was also very loud and outgoing. He wasn't the usual nerd. So I asked him to tutor me in Maths, and he agreed. Every day during break, he would teach me the Maths topic we'd learnt that week. This helped me accomplish two things. First, I was getting better in Maths. Second, I didn't have to run into Alex during break time. If I was hungry, I would send a classmate to buy snacks for me when buying theirs.

By the end of three weeks, I began to do quite well in Mathematics. Then, another complication arose. Chika was beginning to like me, in a romantic way. I noticed it in the way he started treating me with so much respect; sometimes, he would touch my hair for no reason. And he began to insist on carrying my bag after class.

I remember one afternoon, during break, Chika was teaching me the rudiments of permutation. Just as he held my hand and looked into the note, his face so close to mine, I felt the sensation of being watched, and looked up. Alex was standing by the window, looking at us with so much anger. My heart lurched, and I jerked guiltily away from Chika, my heart beating fast.

I could see Alex biting his jaw so hard. He looked like he wanted to strangle me and Chika. Then, he left. I was shaken. The truth was, for a while, I hadn't seen Alex talk to any girl, none at all. Not even Miriam. And I was beginning to get confused. What if I had been wrong? What if nothing had been going on with him and Miriam? What if he really did like me?

Oh, God, it meant I had ruined everything. And I just didn't know how to go to him and apologise. It's not like I was used to talking to him. The only time we had talked, I had embarrassed him in full view of everyone. Would he even forgive me?

The following day, I stood outside his class and waited for him. I had to find a way to talk to him and clear any issues. And even apologise. When he saw me standing outside his class, he left his friends and came to me.

"What is it?" he asked harshly. "Why are you standing here?"

I swallowed. "I wanted to ... um ... wanted to ..."

"If it's Chika you're looking for, I'm sure he's waiting for you in class." Alex gritted his teeth and turned to walk away.

I held his hand, and he turned to look at me. It wasn't anger on his face anymore. He was looking at my lips, like he wanted to kiss them again. I shivered and tightened my grip on him, urging him, pulling him closer. Then, his class teacher came, and the moment was lost.

"Wait for me after class," he said to me.

I let go of his hand and went back to my class.

I had no shame. Truly. If Alex had kissed me right there in front of everyone, I would have allowed him. And I couldn't stop thinking about him. All through class, I was daydreaming. I couldn't wait for the last teacher to leave. Chika noticed me fidgeting and kept questioning me. I made up some lame excuse he didn't believe, but I didn't care. I was going to see Alex again! Nerves and anticipation worked me up.

My last class was the Government class. Of course, the teacher saw me hardly paying any attention and asked me a question which I obviously couldn't answer. His punishment was for me to take the huge load of assignment notebooks to his office. And when I got to his office, he started giving me 'good' advice, on how I should pay attention in class and make better grades.

In a way, I did appreciate his advice, but I was in a rush. I didn't want to keep Alex waiting. After fifteen minutes of valuable lecture which I hardly paid any attention to, I rushed out of his office and ran down to the classroom block. It was empty.

Great! Just one more misunderstanding. Would I ever get what I wanted?

Anyways, I didn't see Alex for a while after. I learned he got sick, again, and had to go home for treatment. Maybe it was a recurring sickness, and in my heart, I prayed it wasn't terminal. I was afraid that though my life was changing for good, something would happen to ruin it.

The strange thing was, though I had some friends now and felt better about myself, I still wasn't happy. You know, happy like I really wanted to be, like I saw in movies and all that. And in the middle of all those new friends, I still felt lonely. Alone. Sometimes, I felt like nothing would ever make me feel really happy. The only time I felt happy was when I was with Alex. And I didn't want him or anybody else to have so much power over me.

It was two weeks later, on Valentine's Day, Chika knelt before me in front of the entire class and presented a flower and a wrapped gift to me. I didn't want to take them; I really didn't. But I also didn't want to embarrass him before the entire class. I had been hoping, even praying, Alex would return before now, but he had not.

So as he knelt there, in front of me, with a look of hope in his eyes, I knew it would be cruel of me to reject him publicly. Amidst cheers and all what not, I accepted the flower and gift, and he stood up and hugged me close.

In my head, I was already planning to call him aside and gently let him down. But right there at the window, I could see Alex, looking in.

***

After the Valentine's Day debacle, we had our mid-term break and went home for half a week from Wednesday to Friday. My school had always been stingy with breaks. I don't think they even wanted to let us out of the school gate except on very compulsory holidays.

So while other schools would have a full week mid-term, mine would give us a half-week mid-term. I still remember my Jss2 Easter break, when we junior boarders crowded the gate and demanded to be let out. I had really thought our massive number would make them let us out, but it didn't happen. And we spent Easter in school.

In my head, I had always imagined romance to be something fun and spontaneous, you know, unplanned and magical. In the movies, they never show how messy things could go in a moment. Maybe we all needed to do rehearsals in real life so everything could go as planned.

Girls have one distinct advantage over boys in the business of romance or love. They never have to bother about doing the asking. Nope. That responsibility falls on the male species. Well, we do have some aggressive females who can take the bull by the horn, but that's few and far between. I never imagined asking a female out would be such a problem for some male, especially the young inexperienced ones.

I had not watched a stage play before, but one evening, I had the ample opportunity to watch a failed romantic one with my older cousin as the star of the show. You see, he was standing outside with me, just gisting and talking generally. I think he was trying to convince me my school was not so bad compared to his. He went to one Police Secondary School, so I guess he was right. I mean, what kind of school had Police as teachers and guards? Not one I would want to attend.

As we were talking, Pamela, a pretty young girl in the area, walked by. Normally, I wouldn't see anything amiss, but suddenly, my cousin lost concentration. He couldn't even complete his sentence. After trying and failing to continue his gist, he started urging me to go back into the house hurriedly. My young mind pieced two and two together and came up with one. So I pretended to enter into the gate and watched him take off after Pamela.

Feeling like a young detective, I followed him as he followed her. I just really wanted to see what he would do or say. So we walked, all three of us, down to Pamela's house, which was a short distance from ours. I started singing the 'three blind mice' poem, you know, because we were all walking blind—Pamela, blind to my cousin's advances; my cousin blind to my trailing him; and me, blind to the fact I would see no action that evening.

I just followed him follow Pamela until she got to her house and entered. Then, he walked past like he was really just going somewhere else. But you and I know the truth—he couldn't summon the courage to talk to her that day. You know, I never knew romance could be hard. The movies make it look so easy. Boy meets girl, they fall in love, everyone's happy, end of story.

But real life is not like this. Things happen, life gets complicated.

Anyways, I was tired of the complications with me and Alex. I decided to just let it go, you know. I got tired of stressing myself out with worries and anxieties. The twists and turns at every corner were making me dizzy, and I was sick of it. Maybe it wasn't such a big deal. I mean, I mustn't date Alex, right? It's not a do or die affair.

Besides, I was sure, by then, he thought of me as desperate. After watching my cousin chase after Pamela, I had concluded the romance business was too messy, too complicated for me. I would just chill all by myself. After all, I'd been all by myself all my life. Nothing had changed.

But all that was philosophy for the bulls because the moment I saw Alex after the mid-terms, my heart flipped over, and all the hopes I'd thought buried came crashing back with overwhelming intensity. I could see us going through life together, getting jobs, raising children, growing old together. But most importantly, my heart felt like a butterfly flying for the first time, my world suddenly coming alive with colour.

I couldn't let anything come between us. I really just needed to know for certain if he liked me or not, and all of this confusion was not helping. I decided to ambush him after class and talk it out.

CHAPTER SEVEN

"So let me get this straight. You saw me talking with Miriam that day, so you got angry and left? And it's why you shouted at me in the dining hall?"

I swallowed and nodded weakly, looking down at the ground with so much focus, you would think my life depended on it.

Alex and I were sitting on the walkway in the classroom block. What he didn't know was how I was extremely uncomfortable, not used to talking about my feelings out in the open. It all happened in my head. Even though I had told Alex "I like you" a thousand times in my head, now that I sat with him facing me, the words just couldn't leave my lips. So I chickened out and told him I wanted to apologise for the dining hall incident.

And I hoped desperately he would be the one to bring up the topic of love, because it sure wouldn't be me. If he did like me, surely, he wouldn't see this as just an apology. Surely, he would take this ample opportunity and ask me out, even ...

"Are you listening?" Alex's voice interrupted.

I nodded, again. I began to hope he wouldn't think me a lizard, the way I was nodding at everything he said.

"At least, you should have come to talk to me about it, instead of just assuming ..."

I rolled my eyes. Great! He was going to give me the same lecture I had given myself a thousand times. Would he get to the part where he says he loves me, too, already? I was anxious, and it was making me impatient.

"So ..." I swung my legs casually against the cement pave way, biting my lips while waiting. I stared at his mouth, willing them to form the words 'I love you.'

It didn't come. He just sat by me, taking deep breaths, until a thought occurred to me. What if he was shy? I mean, really. Now that I think about it, it was possible. I looked down at his hands with my side eye. They were trembling slightly as he held the pavement. His breaths were laboured, like he was uncertain. He was shy. Wow! I never thought.

Smiling, I put my left hand atop his and looked at him directly. He looked at my hand on his, then looked up slowly, at me, and smiled. He liked me, too. He didn't have to say the words. I knew. We smiled at each other. I put my head on his shoulder, and we stayed like this without saying a word, my heart singing happy songs.

The noise from the dining hall signalled the afternoon meal was over, so we left, holding hands and smiling. And it would definitely go as one of the happiest days of my life, you know, the joy you feel when a big dream comes true.

They say you never forget your first love; they have a point.

I used to be so emotional then. I used to feel things so intensely. Sometimes, I wonder where all that passion, that drive went to. I even miss the blissful ignorance. There's something about falling in love without any bad experience getting in the way. It means you get to love freely, without any barrier or fear. It's why first love is unforgettable. Because it was the one and only time you loved freely.

Now, as adults, every time you're about to fall in love, you get afraid and tense. You can't look before you leap because of bad experiences and fear of being hurt. I think I did love Alex that much, with the exuberant intensity of a hormonal adolescent.

Looking back now, I feel somehow foolish and happy. Such love has its consequences. We used to fight a lot. He was always doing things that annoyed me. Like how he was always talking to girls. I hated it. He didn't understand why I always had a problem with it. If only he knew I was just insecure. I had gotten a slice of happiness, and I didn't want anybody to take it away.

Deep down inside, I felt I was not good enough for him, that he needed all those very obviously beautiful girls, and then, this was my biggest fear. I finally had what I wanted, but I was the one driving him away. It took a while before I was able to watch him talk to another girl without feeling intensely jealous. I would just close my eyes, smile, and pretend my mind wasn't boiling with rage.

Not to say Alex didn't have his faults. Sure, he was a good boyfriend. He used to wait for me outside my class every day, then he would carry my bag, and we would walk together. I would be in class, and he would send a junior boy with snacks for me. He was so cute and kind of perfect.

But they say 'like begets like' and 'deep calleth unto deep.' If I was intensely jealous, Alex was insanely jealous. His was paranormal. Really!

He refused to let me sit with Chika anymore. Instead, he made me sit with some other girls in the front row, using the excuse he wanted me to do better in my studies. He didn't like me hanging out with other boys, and he was very calculative about it.

Every morning while I would be coming out for the morning food, he would be waiting for me in the dining. Then, we would walk to the assembly hall together, then to class side by side. There, we would separate to our different classes. Sometimes, I would even feel like he was staring at me from the window. But immediately after the classes, he would be waiting outside my class, and we would walk back to the dining together or just sit and talk with his friends. I felt cool about it, and I know other girls were envious. I didn't realize when Alex became a daily routine.

Ladies always say they don't trust their men because the men give them reasons not to. Alex didn't give me any reason to distrust him. He put so much care, attention, and detail towards me that after a while, the thought of him with other girls didn't bother me.

I didn't realize the extent of his jealousy until the day he saw me walking with Chika to the primary school area to buy snacks. My school had a primary section located just at the back beside the chapel. The snacks from the primary school were much better than the old dry things they sold at our tuck shop.

I met Chika there, and we were walking back together. But Alex didn't see it that way. He didn't even say a word to me. He just went straight to Chika and pushed him down. Yeah, they fought. A small part of me was happy guys were fighting over me—and girls always feel ecstatic when guys fight over them—but the bigger part of me was dismayed.

You remember I told you Alex was tall and kind of had muscles. Well, he used them that day to his advantage, leaving Chika with a broken lip. His friends came and separated the fight, but he didn't stop there. He warned Chika not to come close to me, then grabbed my arm painfully and took me to the chapel. The chapel was locked, so we sat outside on the pavement.

Once we got there, his manner changed drastically. He held my hand tenderly and apologised for fighting. Then, he begged me not to walk with Chika anymore, how he couldn't take it. Underneath, I got the sense he meant Chika and other boys. But you know silly girls and their love of strong men. I simply smiled and said yes. Anything to make my Alex happy.

So I stopped walking with Chika. Inside, I was kind of scared. I knew I was jealous, but not anything like this. But I did love Alex, and if he didn't want me walking with Chika, I was happy to do it. But I did apologise to Chika. He didn't say much, just that he understood.

Love is blind. True. For a while, I was blindly in love, blind to the fact that I stopped walking with any of my male friends, blind to the fact that I didn't notice when other boys stopped talking to me, and blind to the fact that Alex and his friends became the only boys I talked to.

I get the feeling I just really wanted to hold on to him, you know, to hold on to the idea of him, of love.

***

The first time Alex slapped me, we were at the primary school area after class, just hanging out with his friends. We normally did this when we didn't want to go the dining or observe afternoon siesta and prep.

I can't really recall what we were talking about, but I know somehow, it was about Chika. I think that was the time he'd found Chika's notebook in my bag. Yeah, sometimes, he would search my bag. I always thought it was done in jest, you know, to laugh at me for anything he would find, like the day he found clear nail polish and made me paint his nails.

He held the book for a while, quietly staring at it. I didn't even realize what was happening until I turned to ask him a question. He responded with a slap. You know, I had never been slapped before, not even by my mom or my dad.

Everyone became quiet. I could see the shock in his friends' eyes, but I was the most shocked person there. At first, I had to wait for the light to clear from my eyes before I could look at him, holding the notebook accusingly. His friends took the cue and left quietly. He began telling me how he had warned me to stay away from Chika and all that, but I wasn't even hearing him. I was still holding my cheek in shock.

He only stopped talking when he saw the tears in my eyes. The truth is, I had discovered Alex was a sucker for tears. Anytime I really wanted him to do something he wouldn't normally do, I would use the tears trick—don't hate me—but this time, it wasn't a trick.

He bent down to hold me gently. I pushed him off, stood up, and walked away.

We got a new house mistress, a short, dark woman who lived alone in one of the staff quarters near the dining hall. I didn't like her. She would pay impromptu visits to the dorm, search our lockers, and seize any noodles, rice, or food stuff she found.

Normally, other house mistresses would return these contraband items during the mid-term break or at the end of term, but not her. She never returned anything, so the only logical conclusion was she ate them, and I didn't like her. She had a number of annoying traits, too, like her high-pitched voice that grated on my nerves.

Well, you know I'm a quiet, respectful girl. But not to that woman. Somehow, I didn't have any respect for her. I opposed anything she said, blatantly disobeyed her, and basically talked to her like she was my mate.

As a result, I spent a lot of time cutting the grass in front of her office as punishment. Damn! She gave me a lot of blisters. I saw her later, a few years after I'd left school, at a wedding. By then, I was mature enough to feel remorse for my disrespect. I went to meet her, and she greeted me fondly, but she still had that grating voice. Ha ha!

The second time Alex slapped me, my eye turned red, and my cheek got swollen. It was actually two slaps in rapid succession. This time, we were having an argument in class, and he got angry. My pain was not even the slaps, painful as they were. My pain was how he'd slapped me in front of his class. The news spread round school. I could feel pity practically oozing off anybody looking at me. I was so ashamed, I couldn't stay in my dorm. I stayed in Mabel's dorm; in exchange, I had to tell her the juicy story. Remember, she was the school gossip, and she always had a way of finding out things.

Girls rallied around me then, giving me hugs and advice.

"Don't go out with that boy again," they would say, and I would nod in agreement or explode into tears, and they would hug me again. So we made up our minds to end the relationship. They gave me so much strong words of encouragement, I even began to feel smothered. I felt strong, strong enough to end things with Alex.

I lied to the school nurse that I had fallen down the stairs so she could give me something for my eyes. I pitied Alex during that week. The stares of hate and anger he got from all the girls were enough to intimidate anybody. It was like the whole school had rallied against him. I really did appreciate everyone's support then, even though in my ignorance, I failed them the day I forgave Alex, again.

They just couldn't understand the kind of hold he had on me. I couldn't feel complete without him; life felt kind of meaningless, and I missed him so much. The truth is, I didn't plan to forgive him. I was standing strong in my anger and un-forgiveness, ready to break the relationship, but he cornered me. He didn't even apologise. He just looked at my red eyes, and his eyes filled with tears. What did they expect me to do? How could I not love someone who felt my pain like that?

The problem with abuse is, if you don't get out the first time, you fall into a web, a never-ending circle that keeps twirling as long as forever. If I had left Alex the first time, maybe things would have turned out differently. But I can't blame myself. Alex was the embodiment of my dreams, and I didn't want to wake up from that.

I want you to understand something. In my hope how one day, Alex would change, I had begun to believe my love and devotion could ignite this change I wanted. So I stayed with him, even when he pushed me down a granite gutter in anger and I sprained my leg, and when he punched my mouth and broke my lip, loosening a few teeth. I even stayed when he yanked my hair painfully and cut it with scissors.

It was hard to explain. I escaped by telling everyone I had mistakenly got gum stuck in my hair and in a fit of rage, had cut it all off. Not a good story, yes, but at least, nobody bothered me after. I told Alex it was over between us after that incident. He responded with a hard laugh and walked away.

The next morning, he was waiting for me at the dining, acting as if nothing had happened. When I tried to ignore him, he grabbed my arm and held me close to his body. I didn't want a public fight, so I stayed with him all through that day and waited 'til everyone had left before I proclaimed, quite boldly I must say, the relationship was over. Again, he laughed at me and walked away.

The following day, just in front of my class, I heard a commotion, and I rushed outside to the sight of Alex beating up a junior boy. The boy's nose was bloody, his white shirt stained red with blood, and he lay weak on the ground. Still, Alex kept kicking at him until other students intervened. In the midst of the confusion, Alex looked at me and smiled. I think that was the day I truly began to believe Alex was mad, mentally deranged. I never talked about a break up again after that day.

For a while, it felt good being with somebody who couldn't live without me, who was so jealous and possessive, and I must confess, a good kisser. The way Alex touched me ignited me, and sometimes, I would lie awake and dream of him.

But I became afraid of him. I became afraid to look into people's eyes because I knew I would see pity. Tragic love. Despite everything Alex did to me, l still loved him. And every time I said I wanted to break up, it was with the hope the threat would force him to change. Yeah! I was hopelessly romantic.

But I got cured the day he looked at me and smiled, after sending a junior boy to the hospital. He got away with it, too, since nobody told the truth. The whole class covered for him. Some days, I would look at him, handsome, tall, laughing, and being normal, and wish I could stay in that moment forever.

CHAPTER EIGHT

The following term, on my birthday, Alex bought me a white Samsung phone. Of course, this was illegal, but you know, nobody paid attention to their laws. There was always a way around them. Everyone oohed and aahed about the phone; there was quite a number of envy to go around that day. I was happy, hopeful even. There had been no fights for a while now, and everything seemed like it was going back to normal. I began to love him all over again. He put some love songs on my phone and told me to listen to them and think of him.

Everything was going well until ...

That morning was a normal one. Classes were a breeze, and everything seemed fine 'til we went to the dining for the evening meal. I remember we were having beans that evening. It's why when Alex told me to meet him in the classroom block instead of going to the dining, I agreed. So I left the dorm early and went to the classroom block before girls started going to the dining.

That night, I heard things got dangerous. The lights went off in the middle of the meal, and suddenly, everything turned crazy. Like the lights took away sanity. A fight broke out, hot beans flew and burned people's skin and eyes, some girl got stabbed with a fork while other girls were dragged towards the boys' dorm for whatever purposes. Only the timely intervention of a heroic senior girl saved those girls.

Senior Maureen was the only senior prefect in the dining. You know SS3 girls and their pretentious lives.

They never come to the dining when beans were being served. Senior Maureen single-handedly held boys at bay, allowing junior girls to run out of the dining. Then, she went towards the boys' dorm and rescued the other girls before anything could happen. So I heard.

While all the commotion was going on, I was sitting on Alex's lap in one of classrooms, talking a little and laughing a lot. I don't know how, but he'd managed to get some illegal snacks that night. You know what happens when a boy and girl are in love and all alone. We started making out. I told you Alex was a good kisser; really, he was. He kissed me until my lips were bruised, touching me everywhere. Then, my phone rang, the one he'd bought for me, and a message appeared. A love message from some guy named Frank.

To be frank—pun intended—Alex had always been going through my phone every day. But that day, the message was from Mabel's new boyfriend. She got his number from those late night shows where lonely people aired their phone numbers, and since she didn't have a phone yet, she had been using mine to talk to him. And this guy was a deranged disturber, always calling and sending angry messages if she didn't pick up.

Knowing Alex, I warned Mabel to use another person's phone to call him, and she agreed. I don't know which drink made him send the text to my phone, about how I—that is, Mabel—wasn't picking his calls and how much he loved me and all. Fool that he was, he didn't specify any name, just sent the text like the phone belonged to Mabel.

So yeah, Alex was just showering my neck with light kisses when the stupid message came in. Alex, as usual, took the phone to check the message. Let me state here, I was used to this. Anytime my phone rang in Alex's presence, he would answer it. In fact, every morning, he would go through my missed calls, received calls, dialled numbers, inbox and outbox, Facebook activities, etc.

I didn't think anything of it until he removed his hand from my chest and threw the phone to me. From the look on his face, I knew it was something bad. Something really bad. After reading the text, my mind whirled. How would I explain this? It was so incriminating.

"So this is what you do?" Alex asked me quietly, with a calm that surprised me at first.

"It's not what you think …" I tried to explain. "Frank is Mabel's boyfriend, and—"

"Shut up!" he thundered.

There. The roar I was waiting for. I closed my eyes and held my body tight, anticipating a slap or a kick, a blow, anything. It didn't come.

Instead, he walked me back to the dorm and told me to go inside quietly. I could feel the rage pouring through his vibrating skin, the way his hand was drumming against his thigh restlessly like it couldn't keep still, like it needed to do something, smash something. Yet, he watched me walk inside, and it was the first time, since the first slap, that I felt the ray of hope beating down on us.

***

The rest of the term was peaceful and quiet, except for the few strange things that happened. Like when I woke up at about three a.m. and found myself alone in the entire dormitory. I could hear noises downstairs, but fear did not let me leave my bed. Apparently, some girl had seen some spiritual red figures in the dorm and raised an alarm. The whole dorm had rushed outside and then begun a night vigil of intense prayers, worship, and prophecy.

Then one of my classmates, Chiwendu, was stopped by six senior boys after school and asked to kiss all of them. She'd come back vomiting and full of anger, a deep dark rage that followed her like a cloud for weeks. If she'd had a gun, those boys would have been dead.

Even though a few minor skirmishes occurred, Alex never raised his hand to me again. Okay, let me be truthful. After our holidays, Alex came back a born again. I know it sounds like a cliché, but it's the truth. He started going to Sunday services at the chapel, joined the ushering department, and even made me start attending Chapel. Normally, we would go to the Catholic mass because they close early and spend the rest of the afternoon playing around. But things changed.

And I have to admit, he changed me. He called me aside one evening and told me since he's now born again, we wouldn't be kissing or touching or any such romance business and even said, if I wanted, we could end the relationship. I stuck with him. He got me to say the words of repentance, and I did, half-heartedly, just to please him.

Sure enough, he was made the school prefect, and I, a house prefect. People called us the 'Ideal Couple.' We even won the 'Best Couple' award in our last press/social event before we left school.

I hadn't seen Alex since we left school eight years ago. We tried to keep in touch, but lost contact after his parents sent him to school abroad. But every now and then, I would remember him and smile. He'd brought out the voice inside of me, and for that, I was grateful to him.

PART THREE
Chaos

CHAPTER NINE

Uneasy, I tried to concentrate through the service, but it was difficult with Alex sitting just a few feet away from me. Oh, God! How long had I dreamed of meeting him again? Even after secondary school, I never forgot him. He had been my first love. None of my other boyfriends could compare to him. Probably why I could never truly commit to any of them. And now, the same Alex was seated in front of me, tall and handsome as ever. I took deep breaths and calmed my heart.

Soon, Pastor Lanre introduced him as his son, and the whole church went up in applause. Alex took the stage and thanked everyone for their warm welcome. Simon began to signal for us to take the stage behind him. Was Alex going to sing? Interesting. I'd never heard him sing before.

The five of us took the stage and stood behind him in front of our microphones. Then, he started singing.

At first, I stood in surprise. So did the whole church. Alex sang and brought tears to the eyes of many. After the ministration, the entire church burst into applause. Alex bowed and left the altar. I went back to my seat, shivering. The rest of the service passed in a blur, with me unable to concentrate on the sermon. Alex kept filtering through my mind, running around in circles and dancing like an animation.

The service ended, and I put my envelope in the offering basket as Simon signalled for the choir unit to wait behind. I looked over at Alex. He was surrounded by pastors and deacons. Beyond them, other members of the church stood around talking, waiting for a moment to speak with him. He was the new sensation. I averted my gaze and concentrated on Simon's speech. Chioma kept fidgeting and tapping her feet impatiently. I leaned towards her.

"Are you going anywhere special from here?"

She looked and me and flushed, almost like she was guilty of something.

"No. I'm just hungry."

I nodded and leaned back into my seat.

As soon as the meeting was over, half the choir girls rushed into the ladies' convenience, like a herd being steered by invisible hands. What was the rush? I frowned slightly and walked into the convenience.

They were all lined up to the wall-length mirror, touching up their make-up. I grinned, bemused, and walked out to the parking lot, past the crowd surrounding Alex. I would talk to him some other time. That crowd was too much, and my stomach was crying out for food, cooked food, not the snacks sold round the church premises.

Now to get Simon out on time. The man attended so many meetings. I could see him standing with the crowd talking to Alex. Great! He was going to keep me here 'til forever. I should have just brought my car. What is the point of having a car if you can't leave when you want to leave? Why did I depend on Simon so much?

Tapping my foot in agitation, I stood and waited, nodding in greeting as friends and acquaintances passed. Thirty minutes later, I was still standing and waiting. Simon hadn't even had the courtesy to give me his keys so I could sit inside the car, and these heels were killing me.

Feeling terribly like The Hulk, I stormed inside the church. It was a mistake. I don't know if it was the clicking of my heels or just plain Fate. As soon as I stepped through

71

the door, at the same time, Alex turned his face, and our eyes met.

Again, I felt hot and cold, clueless how to react. I smiled nervously and raised my hand to wave. Instead, his face hardened, and he turned away. This was the second time. Why was he doing that? Maybe he didn't recognise me. It had been eight long years ago. Eight years would make my face a blur in his mind. Never mind how his had remained as sharp as a drawing in mine. It would explain his behaviour. Immediately, mortification grabbed me. He probably felt embarrassed about the strange girl constantly looking at him. He may even think me to be brazen.

And why would he remember me, the simple, ordinary girl he'd dated for a short while many years back? I ignored the dark cloud hovering over me. If he didn't recognise me, fine. Then I wouldn't recognise him. I stomped over to Simon standing beside Pastor Osigwe and leaned in to whisper into his ear. Immediately apologetic, Simon handed his keys over, and I left, not sparing a glance at the crowd gathered around the 'newbie.'

What did he mean, anyway? Was I so ordinary, so mundane, that he would forget me? All these years, I had never forgotten even a single moment we had spent together. I treasured his memory so much, I even dream of him occasionally. Now this?

Let it be, Glory. It doesn't matter. It was so long ago. You don't really expect him to remember you.

I took a deep breath and leaned my head back in the car seat.

Simon came out few minutes later. I closed my eyes and leaned back into the car, bottling up my rage and disappointment.

"Are you okay?" he asked, concerned.

I nodded slowly without opening my eyes, pretending exhaustion. He didn't speak again, dropped me off, and zoomed away.

I really shouldn't be feeling this bad. I wasn't even angry anymore. Just disappointed, almost sad. I just never imagined Alex would ever forget me. I thought I'd meant more to him, that our love was to die for, eternal even if only in fond memories.

I turned to and fro all night, falling asleep only in the early hours of the morning, dreaming of a certain young boy with a beautiful voice.

***

"Wake up!"

My mother's voice jolted me awake. I turned and hugged my pillow tighter.

"You're late," she proclaimed.

I jumped up and checked my phone. Seven-thirty. Damn! I had just thirty minutes to get to the office.

Breakfast forgotten, I rushed through my ablutions, forgoing make-up, before rushing up to the car and speeding to work.

I barely made it to the office, dropping my bag on my table before I noticed the low murmur of voices from the manager's office, a door down. My work area was empty. From the low glass wall, I could make out the shape of my colleagues gathered in the manager's office.

The new manager. He was starting today. That was probably the introductory meeting going on there, and I was late. Late on his first day. Maybe I could just sneak in without anyone being the wiser. Before I could wear my jacket, the sound of footsteps and rush of voices told me the meeting was over.

What would the new manager think of a latecomer? I grimaced and sat down. I needed help, more likely favour, loads of it. Maybe an apology would suffice.

I am favoured, I am favoured ... I kept saying, taking deep breaths. Beside me, Georgewill and Juliet went to their work table, ignoring me as I sat with my eyes closed and lips moving.

"Church girl," they chorused together as soon as I opened my eyes, laughing heavily.

"Thank you. I appreciate," I said, bending my head and arranging my table.

"So, Glory, upon all your churchy churchy life, you still come late today. Kai!" Georgewill said, smacking his hands together and holding arms over breast, like a market woman getting ready to gossip.

I rolled my eyes and glared at Juliet, daring her to say a word in support of Georgewill.

She laughed and waved her hands in surrender. "Georgewill, please leave her. Maybe she had a vigil last night."

I ignored their smirks and went to the balcony for a moment alone. It was the only quiet place in this office, giving me the solitude necessary to pray. Rushing off to work meant my prayer time had been cut short.

The honk of angry drivers, speeding cars, pedestrians, hawkers, and hard swerves rolled off the balcony, almost a distraction if I didn't treasure it. Here is my favourite place in the office, especially back when Mr. Bode, the former manager, was around. Oh, I have made so many prayers here, and as I stood, humming a worship song, the peace I was searching for suddenly came down. I said a short prayer and made to leave.

And stopped. Alex. He was just standing there, right beside the door, wearing a deep blue suit and looking as handsome as ever. He looked like he had been standing there a while.

Where had he come from?

I remembered my squeaky clean face and wished I had taken the time to just apply concealer, foundation, anything.

"You ... what are you doing here?"

He didn't say anything. Just turned and left. What would Alex be doing in my office?

Maybe he finally remembers you and came to see you.

My heart jumped at the thought. But even if he did remember me, why would he come to my office when he could easily see me in church on Thursday?

He probably couldn't wait that long to see you.

Ha! No! If he had come to see me, he wouldn't leave without talking to me.

There was only one reason, not fantasy, why Alex would be in my office on Monday morning.

Business, a rational part of me said. He could only be here for some work issue. I took a deep breath to calm my nerves, ignored the pang of disappointment in my chest, and went back into the corridor leading to my office.

As I walked past the manager's office, I glanced in, just to see if he/she was now around so I could go apologise and introduce myself.

Another shocker. Alex was sitting with a dark, short, but good-looking man, my supposed new manager. I quickly bent my head and passed, not wanting the new manager to see me until I'd had a chance to apologise for coming late.

Who falls in love with someone they have never talked to? Me.

Who falls in love with someone who didn't even know their name? Me.

And now, I was determined not to fall in love with the same person again.

Whatever business he came for would end.

I whistled while drawing out some papers and concentrated on registering new clients. Damn. Some handwritings were so bad, they just might make me need glasses later on in life. I brought a particularly bad sheet to my face, trying to ascertain if the letter I was seeing was 'g' or 'r'. How g and r would look alike was something I didn't even bother trying to comprehend.

It was the scraping of chairs that alerted me. Georgewill and Juliet would only be standing up so quickly for the new manager.

Hastily, I dropped my paper sheet and stood up to face the man I had seen in the manager's office earlier.

"Good morning, sir." I extended my arm for a handshake, hoping he wouldn't mention my lateness to work.

He didn't mention it as he took my hand in a firm grip. He also hadn't come in alone.

Alex. He stood behind him, so handsome and so quiet. My nerves began acting up, leaving me not knowing how to keep my arm still or my knees from shaking. Damn. Why did he have this much effect on me?

Because you allow it, the voice in my head replied.

Right. Here I stood, barely able to contain myself with just standing when all I wanted to do was run into his arms and hold him so tight. While he stood there, unaffected and oblivious, smiling at Juliet and Georgewill with his perfect white teeth.

Great! Now I was jealous of the people he smiled at.

The new manager, Mr. Ade, had finished introducing himself and inspecting the office, but he was saying something else that snapped me right back to attention, something about a supervisor.

What supervisor?

It couldn't possibly be.

It was. Mr. Ade was smiling as he introduced Alex as the new department's supervisor.

What happened to Mrs. Ambode?

"Mrs. Ambode has resigned," he said in answer to the question in my head.

Alex was smiling and giving handshakes to Juliet and Georgewill. My hands were all sweaty and shaky. If he shook them, he'd know how badly affected I was by his presence.

Surreptitiously, I wiped my hands on my skirt and took calming breaths to relax my quivering bones. What was the point, anyways? He doesn't remember me. Why kill myself with swirling emotions and turmoil for someone who had no idea who I was?

Suddenly, the walls surrounded me. It was happening again. Even after eight years, somehow, I had become the wallflower again.

Annoyed, I didn't smile as he approached and held out his hand. I stared at the offending hand a bit before slowly bringing mine out, sending a silent prayer it was steady and firm.

I don't know about that. I mean, the moment he covered my hand with his, it all came crashing down—my steely resolve, my hard glare. I felt alive, like I had finally come home. I melted, and all I wanted was to fall at his feet and beg him to remember me, to love me again.

Please love me, I pleaded inside my heart.

Even though it took a few seconds, it felt like a lifetime to me, and I had to remember he was speaking to me.

"You must be Miss Owhor," he was saying, his face set in a neutral expression.

"Yes. Good morning, Al— sir"

I had almost called him by his name. Damn.

He didn't seem to notice the near-mistake, either, just went right back to Mr. Ade, talking as they left.

Alex, my new supervisor. Not only would I have to see him every day, I'd have to talk to him about everything except the one thing I needed to talk to him about.

Just tell him who you are.

No. No way. If he didn't remember me, then I meant nothing to him.

And maybe he was right to not remember me. After all, it was just a teenage romance, something to be easily forgotten. Something nobody concerned themselves with. Why was I making it seem too deep?

Surely, people must meet their adolescent boyfriends and not go over the moon because of it.

Grow up, I cautioned myself and sat down. If anything, I wouldn't be that weak, pitiful, pathetic girl mooning over Alex again. No. I am not a teenager anymore. I can handle this.

Feeling infinitely confident, I sat down and went back to work with a snap, trying desperately to ignore Juliet and Georgewill's gossip, but my ears caught some of it.

"Did you know he graduated with distinction?" Georgewill was saying to Juliet.

"Bookish," she replied and promptly left the office.

She came back with her hair looking newly combed and arranged, her lipstick a bit more pouty.

Alex always brought this kind of reaction in women.

Suddenly, I was glad I had worn no make-up. I wouldn't join the line of girls desperately trying to catch his eye. I mean, what was the appeal, anyway?

How he'd schooled abroad? Or his tall, handsome features, his broad smile, and dimples?

Whatever! There are a thousand and one Nigerian schooled men who are successful and handsome, too.

Yet, you have none.

I ignored the voice and snapped the form I held close.

How could I concentrate like this? He hadn't even been back for up to a week, and I already felt like my life was turning upside down.

Even the church that was my refuge had been contaminated by him.

Alex, Alex, Alex ... I fumed and went to the balcony.

Why was I so angry?

Maybe you don't want him to know you're still single and shamefully still have feelings for him.

Ha! Like I care. So what if I was twenty-seven and single? I wasn't the first, neither was it a crime. And I didn't harbour any feelings for him. I mean, I'd be a fool right? You can't love someone who doesn't remember you.

He just had to come back at the time I was feeling terribly single and lonely. Horrible timing.

Lord, what do I do? I asked over and over again as I paced.

When I heard nothing in reply, I went back to the office. I'd talk to God about it later. He'd surely give me an answer and a strategy. Better yet, He'd send me someone, a real life boyfriend/fiancé/husband. Anything.

To be frank, I was getting tired of this single business. I just hadn't been interested in the whole boyfriend business for a while. Maybe because I hadn't felt something other than friendship for any man in a long time. It just seemed like an inconvenient bother.

But now, I was starting to feel edgy about it. Maybe it was time for that in my life. Maybe it's why I had been feeling disgruntled and unhappy for a while now. I smiled. It really seemed like now would be a good time for a relationship.

I knew the minute it hit closing hour because I kept staring at the wall clock, willing it to run faster so I could leave here and breathe easy. I grabbed my bag and went straight to my car. For as long as it took, I'd avoid him.

Why?

Because he didn't remember me. Weak, I sat in my car, my head on the steering wheel as I came face to face with the force behind my anger.

He didn't remember me.

Had I meant so little to him? I had loved him so completely, in a way I hadn't been able to love any other person. Why was I so forgettable?

The tears rose in my eyes, and my shoulders heaved. Even now, I still felt like the invisible girl from secondary school. Would I always struggle with this?

I would be strong tomorrow, but today? Today, I would cry and eat all the ice cream I wanted. Just as I drove out of the parking lot, I saw He-Who-Must-Not-Be-Named emerging from the office, talking with Juliet, who was all smiles.

He can talk to all the girls in the entire world. I couldn't care any less.

Liar.

CHAPTER TEN

By the time I arrived home, I knew something had gone wrong. Jaja was standing outside, smiling like someone enjoying a show, my mom beside him with an open bag filled with shoes.

Uh oh!

Nene had returned.

My mother didn't even let me drop my bag. She turned to me as Jaja greeted.

"Imagine that ungrateful, rumour-spreading girl. As if I need her here. Did I even ask her to come here? Pack your things and leave immediately!" she screamed into the house.

I held her as she bent to lift a bag and haul it outside the gate. She was sending Nene out. Or Nene had come to get her things. Nene came out, carrying a red tote. She smiled as she saw me, smiled at Jaja, picked up the bag, and left.

"Nonsense," my mother called out and stormed inside to her room, tapping her foot wildly in agitation.

By the time I had dropped my bag and turned around, there she was. I knew it. Now, she would spend hours, spewing and complaining and talking, and I'd have to put up a semblance of attention when I'd really be thinking of everything from work to choir to Alex to Simon to God, and everything in between.

I roused myself to hear her say,

"And your father does not even care. I swear he gets more absent-minded every day. Is it too much for him to open his eyes and see, to really see how his people just try to undermine me always?"

"Ah ah." I dropped my phone, where I had been playing Temple Run. "You know Daddy will always support you, right or wrong. And when he does bring his mind back to Earth, you know he does love you."

It's true. My parents are not the typical Nigerian couple out there. Maybe my dad's years in a London university helped. It's not strange to see them sipping champagne and watching CNN together. Their last anniversary, my dad had managed to take two weeks off, and they went to Kenya, taking pictures of everything, even the ceiling of their hotel room.

Occasionally, at night when they stay up late, they'd cuddle together on the couch, much to Jaja's consternation.

"Why can't they act like normal parents?" he'd ask anytime he caught them kissing.

I'd long since gotten used to it.

This Nene issue, I knew, was just beginning.

***

I spent the next two days coming up with ingenious ways to avoid Alex. And it worked. Whenever I bumped into him, I'd call out a hasty greeting and dash off to the nearest office. Once, I nearly entered the men's convenience in a slip of attention and a healthy dose of runningscobia. Yup, I just came up with that.

Whenever he came to talk to the office, I'd let Juliet and Georgewill do the talking and questions. Juliet was happy to do it. Her skirts kept getting shorter, and her lipstick more pronounced. I wondered how short her skirt would be in two weeks' time. This was just three days.

Conveniently, I ignored the fact he'd be in church on Thursday for the midweek service. It didn't mean much to me, anyway. I'd avoid him, as usual, and only recognise him as my boss in the office.

Service was a breeze. I avoided bumping into him until it was over and I was ready to leave.

My intention was to say hi, just to recognise him as my boss in the office, but of course, things didn't go as planned.

First of all, he was surrounded by pastors, ushers, and basically everyone wanting to meet the Senior Pastor's eligible son. That included a lot of choristers, ushers, women, and even aged men with single daughters.

I almost got angry at the sight. Why were they all acting like he was a god? Wasn't that making a mockery of our religion?

"Why are you frowning?" Simon asked as he came up from behind me.

"Nothing. Just had a tough day in the office."

"Alright. I have to speak to Alex. Wait for me, please." He started to leave, then came back with a calculating look on his face. "You haven't met Alex yet, have you?"

I smiled nervously. There's no way I could hide the truth. Sooner or later, he'd find out.

"I've actually met him. He's my new supervisor." I said it casually, hoping he wouldn't notice anything amiss.

God bless his soul, he didn't.

"Really? Wow. Alright, then, let's go say hi," he urged and practically grabbed my arm and led me forward.

They exchanged pleasantries before Alex turned to me.

"Good evening," I said to him.

He smiled back, making my heart jump. "Miss Owhor, how are you doing?"

To an outsider, he sounded normal, casual even, but I knew he was acting all stiff. I stiffened up, too, feeling like a soldier and probably looking like one standing at full attention.

"I'm fine." I took a step backward, positioning Simon between us as they talked.

"You should think about joining the choir," Simon was saying to him.

Joining what? I glanced at Simon in shock. Not only would I have to face him in the office and in church, but in choir, too?

"No ..." Alex said pointedly. Something about the way he said it made me look up.

He was looking directly at me—at my frown, I must say, and he was frowning right back.

Had he noticed my reaction when Simon had asked him to join the choir? Suddenly guilty, I turned my eyes away. The choir was not my personal property. He could join if he wished to.

I was getting tired of hide and seek, anyways. I mean, it was something that shouldn't mean anything to me. Why should it bother me so much?

He's just a guy. I can't turn my life upside down just because of a harmless and meaningless teenage flirtation.

Okay. Be mature about this. I wouldn't be so antagonistic and dispassionate about him anymore. I'd just treat him as a casual acquaintance. Maybe this was a warning, telling me to let go of my past and move into the future.

How could I hope to love someone else when my heart was already occupied by a memory?

I left the crowd surrounding Alex and walked to my car. If Simon kept me here longer than fifteen minutes, I'd go home without him.

The man loved meetings so much. Sometimes, he'd just hang around talking to pastors.

Maybe he wanted to be a pastor someday. I smiled at this thought. Pastor Simon. It had a nice ring to it. I could totally see him standing at the pulpit and preaching so passionately, jumping up and down and gesticulating wildly.

It'd be good for him.

"Glory."

The voice came behind me, but I knew who it was— because my heart jumped, not with fright, but with recognition.

And he sounded just like my Alex, the one I loved, not the hard, grown-up voice he'd been using.

I couldn't bring myself to turn. My body kept shaking, and my legs turned to jelly instantly.

"Say something. Turn," I whispered to myself.

It was happening again. How was it that every time it came to Alex, I'd be reduced to this painfully shy teenager? Why did he have so much power over me?

I cleared my throat because a little green monster had wrapped his hands around my throat, making it close up.

"I know you're waiting for your boyfriend. I just have to ask, do you really not recognise me?"

My heart leaped. He knew me. He hadn't forgotten.

He hadn't forgotten.

Turn around. Say something.

Still, I remained immobile.

"You don't want your boyfriend to know about us, right? Or you just plain don't remember me?"

Damn it. Say something, Glory. Turn around. Do something. Anything.

I could see Simon walking towards me. Alex must have seen him, too, because he laughed harshly, and then, I felt his hands on my arm.

He pulled my arm and began to lead me towards the generator house, his strides quick and brisk. I followed because somehow, I knew he would have dragged me if I didn't.

He pulled me to the wall and covered me with his body, placing his hands on the concrete beside my head and successfully locking me in.

His face was close—so close, I could see the brown flecks in his eyes. I could smell his musky scent.

"Tell me you really don't remember me ..."

He was too close, almost overpowering me.

"Alex," I said simply.

I couldn't say anything else.

Something in his eyes changed. The anger fled, and a new light filled his eyes, like recognition. He knew I hadn't forgotten.

I looked up at him. Then, his eyes looked down, to my lips.

Suddenly, they felt dry, parched. I brought out my tongue and licked my lips, to wet them.

He made a small sound, then brought his head down, his lips almost touching mine.

My phone suddenly rang, the light flashing in my pocket.

Sanity returned, and we jerked away from each other.

What is wrong with you, Glory? Would you really kiss a guy out here, even in church?

I felt ashamed. How would I explain this to God, how I had been so overcome with lust, I almost kissed Alex right in church?

I turned and fled.

Simon was standing by my car, obviously waiting for me.

"Where did you go?" he asked, concerned.

"The convenience," I replied, keeping my head down to avoid his eyes. Surely, he'd be able to see my shame; it was written all over me.

"Are you okay?"

I nodded and began to open my door. My hands shook so bad, the keys slipped and fell to the interlocked ground.

Simon bent down to retrieve them. With one knee on the ground, he looked up at me, the light from the security lamps illuminating his face.

Then, he stood up and opened the door.

I saw quick movement, towards the generator house. Alex stood there, watching us.

Quickly, I entered my car, and Simon closed the door.

"We'll talk tomorrow," he said gravely.

I didn't see the cars or the road as I drove home and fell with exhaustion on my bed. Alex hadn't forgotten. He remembered me.

My heart couldn't stop dancing. I hummed as I showered, said a short prayer, and fell into a dreamless sleep.

CHAPTER ELEVEN

The next day, I was in the middle of analysing a really bad handwriting when a text from Simon came in, asking me to meet him at the fast food close to my office during lunch hour.

Probably some church activity. Should I talk to him about the whole Alex thing? It couldn't hurt. Besides, I was getting tired of carrying it all by myself. I needed to talk about it, let it out. He could offer some new perspective.

I had avoided him all morning, but we had a meeting immediately after the lunch hour, and I'd have to see him. I needed new perspective, preferably a guy's perspective, and Simon could provide that. All you do, diary, is listen, watch, and keep quiet without proffering solutions or giving me feedback.

I never anticipated what happened next. I mean, there I was, complaining about the lack of romance in my life, feeling a bit invisible, and in the space of days, the story changed.

Simon was hardly himself throughout lunch. He kept fidgeting, and I noticed he was sweating despite the air conditioner blowing cold air right in front of our table.

Spaghetti is my favourite meal, and I enjoyed this particular one. I ignored the many times he'd open his mouth and start to say something, then think better and stop.

He excused himself and went to the bathroom as I rounded up the spaghetti on my plate. The food here is great. Maybe I should check out new pasta recipes online, to add to the ten recipes I already know. God, can I get any more boring?

Simon's phone vibrated, and because the phone faced me, I could see the caller. Kelechi drummer. I don't know why we save people's names in strange ways, and I am most guilty. Sometimes, going through my contacts, I don't know half the names because what I thought was a clever way to remember the person becomes mumbo jumbo weeks after. Who the heck is Joe snuffer? I had wrestled with that one for weeks.

The phone stops vibing, and it's when I see it, the Word document titled *I Love You, Glory!*

Normally, I would avert my eyes, but somehow, seeing my name made it hard. I grabbed the phone and saw the Word document composition.

I have known you for years and have never uttered a word.

How then do I tell you that every time you're near, my heart skips a beat?

How do I tell you that I've loved you for so long? Will you believe me?

This love stole its way into my heart.

I woke up one morning and there you were, so tightly lodged inside my heart,

I knew I was lost in you.

What?

Somehow, I should have known. They say a boy and girl can't be just friends. Feelings must creep in. Don't get me wrong. I like Simon. I love him like a brother, which is what he has been to me since the first day I became born again in church.

He had been the one to counsel me, and we had developed an easy friendship from there. He had really helped me with my faith especially those times I wanted to give up, like when I began clubbing excessively in my third year in school, or when I thought smoking shisha was okay, or when I began dating a cultist because he was super handsome and I loved his devil-may-care attitude, or when I— Okay, you get it. In one sentence, I could say he was the one who helped me stand firm in my faith, and soon, we became pretty close.

It helped how he lived in the same street, and he began to pick me up and drop me off from church regularly. Even when my dad bought me my car and I started working, it only became natural he'd continue to take me to church Saturdays and Sundays.

Okay. Now that I think about it, I should have seen it coming. We couldn't be any closer if he was a girl and we had sleepovers.

Everyone had thought we were in a relationship, and we'd both laughed over it. Or had he? Maybe I was the only one who'd seen it like a joke.

As he came back and said he had to leave, I wracked my brain, trying to remember if he had laughed when people had said we were dating. I couldn't come up with anything. All I kept seeing was a forced smile.

He left, and I smiled awkwardly at him. He had no idea I had seen his love note. To me.

And Fate wasn't on my side. You can guess who I ran into coming out of the fast food.

Sure enough, Alex stood there as I ran past. I'm sure he must have seen Simon there and put two and two together because he kept gritting his teeth during the department meeting. He always did that when angry. I really couldn't concentrate much 'til I heard him call my name as if from a distance.

"Care to share what you were thinking about?" he asked, a sneer on his face.

Mortified I had been caught, I'm sure I must have turned beet red. I just cleared my throat and shook my head.

"No. Sorry, sir. Please continue," I said, abashed.

"Please try to keep your mind here, now, in this meeting," he said, so angrily, something snapped in me.

What did he think, anyways? That he could talk to me anyhow just because he was now my boss?

I gritted my teeth and stomped my feet in anger until the meeting ended. I stood up quickly, making sure my chair made a grating noise, and went back to my office.

All I could think about was Simon, in love with me. How? When had this all started?

Oh, God! I had never even thought about it remotely. I always assumed he'd be my friend always.

Georgewill and Juliet came in at the same time, laughing together.

"Glory, what was that? What happened during the meeting?" Juliet asked in an offhand manner as she sat on her desk.

I looked at her skirt and shook my head again. She was still wearing them really short.

"I just got a bit distracted," I said vaguely.

Suddenly, I looked at her raptly. Maybe she could help.

"Umm, have you ever been asked out by a close friend?" I said, bending down towards her table so Georgewill wouldn't hear. He was the biggest gossip in the entire office.

Juliet smiled. "Boy or girl?"

"Boy," I said, angry at the question.

She laughed and threw her hand at me. "Don't be angry. You didn't specify."

"Well, have you?"

She narrowed her eyes. "Are you asking me if it's a good idea to date a friend?"

I nodded impatiently. "Yes."

"It depends. It's hard to start loving a platonic friend in that way. But I think it's better to date a friend, you know, someone you've been friends with. Or so I've heard."

Do I have any romantic feelings for Simon?

He's handsome, I know. All the girls in the choir at one time or the other developed feelings for him. Sometimes, they would come up to me, asking for information. One of them had boldly asked me upfront if I was his girlfriend. When I told her no, she had asked me quite politely to shift and make room for the interested ones.

Simon had never expressed interest in any of them, anyways. He acted like he didn't know there were ladies, interested ones, in the choir. Some of them got the message pretty quickly. The more stubborn ones got rejected so harshly, they never came close again.

Has he been in love with me all this while?

If he had, then I've been blind for years.

"Glory, is Simon asking you out?" Juliet asked.

Unfortunately, Georgewill's ears picked this up, and he squealed. "Finally, Glory, you and Simon are now together. I told you. I told you. Now you owe me," he said to Juliet.

"He's only asking. She has not said yes yet," Juliet shot at Georgewill, who stopped and thought about it.

"True," he said, and sat down, disappointed.

They'd been betting on me and Simon being together? Had everyone seen this except me?

Suddenly angry, I stood up and went to the balcony, carelessly wiping the tears falling.

If Simon has loved me all this while, then I've treated him quite shabbily.

God, how did I never notice?

Things would never return to normal. Simon had irrevocably changed my life. Damn it. I didn't need this now, not when I was still trying to sort out my feelings for Alex.

That night, as I lay on my bed, my phone vibed. I got a message simply saying, "Sorry about what happened in church the other evening. Alex"

Alex. Why was he apologising for almost kissing me? Did he regret it?

Regretting it was the honourable thing to do, not to be happy and blissful like me. When did I become so wanton, that I didn't feel any guilt for almost kissing an old ex on church premises? And I wanted it to happen again.

But Simon ... do I love him?

I honestly didn't know. I felt numb inside, neither hot nor cold. What if I loved him, too, somewhere inside my heart? Why was I so attached to him?

I went everywhere with him, everywhere. I couldn't imagine life without Simon.

Then how about Alex?

What did I feel for Alex? Love or lust?

I groaned and tossed all night, sleep evading my eyes.

CHAPTER TWELVE

I thought I could safely evade Alex the rest of the following week until I could figure things out. But he didn't give me the chance.

As I sat down in the small kiosk of the lady who sold bole´, roasted plantain, and fish, he came and sat next to me so naturally, as if he had been doing so for years. I ignored my wildly beating heart, accepting it as a normal reaction whenever Alex was near. I didn't pay attention to my trembling hands and shaking legs. *Control yourself, Glory*.

"So this is your second lunch hour hide-out," he said, smiling; a nice smile without any heat, any subtle hint underneath.

"Just when I want some *bole´*," I said, hoping my smile was straight and my lips were not shaking like a leaf during harmattan season.

"So, what do you recommend?"

I pointed to some already roasted plantains and fish, which the seller promptly put in a dish and poured stew atop.

"God, I missed this so much," he said and dug in.

How could he eat with so much appetite? Wasn't his lip immobile, his hands trembling like mine?

No. He was smiling and concentrating on his meal. How could he be so unaffected? Where was the passionate man who'd almost kissed me before?

I couldn't eat, just pushed my food around.

"Listen, I want to apologise for my behaviour the other night in church. I know you received my text, but I have to do it in person. I'm sorry for my rude behaviour. I hope we can still be friends in spite of it?"

If we were animated characters, my mouth would have been hanging open. Why was he been so formal?

I must have mumbled yes because he smiled at me, a friendly, aloof smile holding no hint of emotion, like I was an object he was fond of or an old friend. He then paid for his meal, mine included, and walked away with a, "See you at the office."

I couldn't ponder much. Lunch hour was almost over, and I hurried into the office, feeling broken and unreal, like I was in a movie, a bad one, at that. Whoever was writing my script needed to do more work. Why wasn't I happy?

Alex was being cool and distant, which is what I wanted, right? To be free from the hold of his memory. I mean, we can still be friends. Friends move on.

Yeah, and friends don't act all love-struck when with other friends. I didn't see him when he left, either, even though I craned my neck looking at the exit door constantly. Maybe he was working late. As the new supervisor, he must be under a lot of pressure to perform, to show his worth.

My heart lurched at the thought of him working so hard. Did he even have any friends yet? I hadn't seen him with anybody unrelated to church and work. Poor baby.

Suddenly, the image of holding his hands and massaging his shoulders popped into my mind. I wanted to hold him, make sure he eats properly, kiss him goodnight.

Get over it, Glory. I snapped my office door closed and marched straight to my car. For all I knew, he may be out with friends, winding down, or with a girlfriend. The thought of another girl in his life was a painful one.

Simon was parked outside my gate when I arrived home. Oh, yeah, we had a plan to catch up. How could I be normal around him when I knew how he felt about me? Wouldn't it be cruel?

I drove into my compound and met my mother pounding yam in the kitchen.

"Simon is waiting for you," she called out.

How did she know he was outside the gate? If I refused to go with him, she'd hound me until the truth falls out. Knowing my mum, she'd be exceedingly glad. Lately, her subtle hints about the lack of a man in my life had lost their subtlety and were bordering on loud.

I dropped my bag, showered quickly, and changed into jeans and a simple top. Quickly, I rushed outside.

"How was the office?" he asked, whistling as he drove away. We were going to my former university campus.

Sometimes, on those boring evenings, we'd drive to the campus, order fries and *suya*, and just sit and talk for a while. Simon is a good listener, and I'm a good talker.

I looked at him, searching for signs of his love, anything.

He turned to me. "What is it?"

"Nothing," I mumbled. He looked and acted so normal. How could he?

I decided to test the waters. If I tell him about another guy, his reaction would confirm it. I mean, he would get jealous and forbid me from seeing other guys, right? I decided to hide Alex's identity and just tell him the story. No need dredging up bad situations.

We were sitting on the grass, munching on peppered *suya* when I asked him.

"I ran into my secondary school boyfriend recently. And I think I still like him."

"This from the girl who's not looking to date but court." He smiled.

I watched closely. His eyes didn't darken; he didn't clench his fists or grind his teeth like one jealous or angry. In fact, he was looking at me expectantly, for a reply.

"Well, I said I'm not ready to date, but it doesn't stop me from feeling ... stuff."

"Really?" Simon looked at me with interest, so casual and cool.

Where was the jealousy?

I squirmed under his gaze. "I do have crushes now and then."

I gripped my fries and chewed sternly.

"Hmmmm. And what do you do when these feelings emerge? And over whom ... anybody I know, in church?"

"No ..." I said quickly, giving off an awkward laugh. I slapped his shoulder, a casual gesture I do so many times. "Why are you being so inquisitive, acting like you've never had a crush before?"

Now was the perfect time for him to tell me. I held my breath and waited. He didn't give me any looks with hidden meanings. Love didn't light up the fire in his eyes.

"First, you must determine if you actually do have feelings for him or if you're acting based on left-over feelings and good memories." He bent his neck and raised his eyebrows, waiting for me to nod and comprehend.

All these feelings for Alex, could they be left-over feelings? We hadn't officially broken up. When he'd been travelling out to school, he had given me his address, his mail, and a ring.

Oh my gosh, I had totally forgotten. Alex had given me a ring, to remember him by. Yes, I recall it now.

Then, his parents had been living in Lagos, and after graduation, he had moved back to Lagos instead of his uncle's house he normally spent short holidays in. He had managed to convince his parents to send him on a short holiday with his uncle in Port Harcourt.

It was the first time we were seeing each other after graduation. We had gone out to lunch in a fast food, and we'd stayed and talked 'til evening. His beard had now been growing all over his jaw, and I remember being enthralled with the changes, and the smell of his deodorant. Towards evening, I'd had to return home before my mother got back from a wedding. He'd walked me home, and just before we got to my gate, he had pulled it out of his pocket. His hands had been shaking as he'd told me to wear it and remember him until he returned.

How could I have forgotten? Whatever happened to the ring, anyways?

"Well ..." Simon said, looking at me strangely.

I had been quiet for a while.

"I don't think its left-over feelings. It's intense."

"Okay. That's good. Then you have to ... what do you normally do when you have a crush?"

"I pray."

"Pray?"

"Yes. You may find this hard to believe, but I have crushes a lot. I trip for fine boys easily, though the problem is that once I know them, it disappears. If I don't pray and control myself, my feelings would lead me into a relationship which might end in disaster. Remember, no time for dating, just courtship."

"Then do the same. Simple." He popped a piece of fried potato into his mouth, pleased with his solution.

Men! In his calculations, it was as simple as that. And for one who had written such a beautiful love poem to me, he seemed nonplussed by it all.

"I just want to enjoy the feeling of being in love for a while," I said finally.

"Seriously? What does it mean? You want to date him for a while?"

"No. I just ... want to have ... this crush for a while. It's been so long since I liked somebody. I miss it. I don't want to take it too seriously. Besides, like you said, it could just be left-over feelings that will fade away in days."

"You must really like this guy."

The blood rushed to my face. Luckily, melanin covered up my blush, and I playfully jabbed his shoulder.

When I got back home, my mom was sitting on her bed, facing the dresser and staring into thin air. As I went in and greeted, she replied with, "Your father has called a family meeting, about the Nene situation. Apparently, she has been telling the whole village how she can't live with me because I am too wicked. And your father wants to jump in and save the situation."

Her words were full of distaste.

She may be dreading it for other reasons, but all I see whenever we have these family meetings are the stacks of food I'd need to prepare, serve to the gazillion relatives, and clean up afterwards. My dad's family is huge as his father had five wives. I have so many cousins, sometimes, it's hard to keep count. Family meetings to my mom mean a lot of talks aimed at resolving issues. To me, it meant working as a hostess and trying to call everybody by the right name and greet each aunt, uncle, and relative properly to avoid World War III between them and my mom.

"Your father thinks these meetings help to solve anything. I am not lifting a hand to help him," she declared and promptly rose up to go sleep in her husband's room.

Uggghhh!

This means all the preparation would be left to me, like I don't have enough on my plate already.

***

Alex maintained a cool and aloof politeness to me the following couple of days. He'd smile and ask about my day, talk about work, and go back quietly to his office. Even in church, he'd smile at me, say goodbye, and walk away. Was I invisible again? And why wasn't I happy with the way things were going?

On Friday, my father waylaid me, just before I drove off to work. Apparently, my mom had refused to cook for the family meeting tomorrow, and I was next in line. I groaned as I took the money.

When would I find time to go to the market during work, except, of course, lunch hour? Great!

Then, I'd still have to go to service in the evening and get back home to prepare for the meeting.

That was until I remembered one of the senior girls back in school who'd recently started a home delivery service for market goods. She used to be one of my novel suppliers back in school, and I gave the business a ring and placed orders. Sure, it would be a little bit more expensive, but today, it was a lifesaver. Besides, I admire her business. In fact, going to Facebook, I see a lot of friends are now entrepreneurs, and sometimes, I feel green with a need to start my own thing. Not that I don't love my job.

Okay, so my dad helped in getting this job, but I am totally competent in it. I know this because I have stellar reviews from my boss, and I will soon be up for promotion.

It's just, watching most of them with their businesses, I feel like there's something I should offer the world.

And just as if Pastor Lanre knew my line of thought, the evening service sermon was on entrepreneurship and business, and then, he said something that made me smile, and I realised I have good capital already from my huge savings, helped by the fact I don't pay rent because, you know, my mom will kill me if I move out except to my husband's place, and I have free food. I hand over a portion of my salary to my mom and dad.

They, in turn, put it in savings for me. I know because I overheard them once when I eavesdropped on them. Don't look at me like that. Everybody eavesdrops on their parents, you know, to know if they're having issues, if they've settled it and stuff like that.

Sometimes when I'm too exhausted, I ask Jaja to keep his ears open for clues. And my parents don't help issues, either. They leave their door open most times when discussing sensitive topics. It's how Jaja knew that even though he'd lost a month's allowance for getting caught kissing a girl in school, Dad was proud of him.

Honestly, I don't know what it is with men. If it was me caught kissing a guy in secondary school, my dad would freak out. Seriously.

Thank God for boarding schools, anyway. It's like a whole different life you live in school your parents never know about. I mean, they think it's all about studying and classes. Oh. If only they knew.

Okay, I'm digressing too much. Where was I? Yes. In church. Service was a blast, but then, things turned sour.

As usual, I was getting into Simon's car after the service to sit and wait for him when I spied Alex coming out of the building with Chioma. They were smiling and talking so animatedly, I could tell something was up.

As I watched, the book in her hands fell to the ground, and Alex promptly bent to pick it up. To others, it may have been an innocent gentlemanly act, but not to me. Alex was the perfect gentleman, but the way he held the crook of her elbow and steered her away from running into a group of elderly matrons, the way he smiled at her, his beautiful smile that melted my heart, I knew he was being different with her. He had maintained a cool, restrained, but friendly aloofness with the girls in church. Why was he suddenly being over-friendly with Chioma?

They continued walking 'til they got to his car. Somehow, I should have known, but I still managed to be surprised when Chioma got in.

He was taking her home.

The past days of easy friendship had been hard, but now, I was reading the signs clearly. Alex was interested in Chioma. I felt so betrayed, my heart burning inside of me.

He drove past Simon's car, and in that flash of a moment when his car was beside Simon's, he looked right at me, a look that sent shivers down my spine, like he was angry at me.

Even after he'd driven off, I remained shaken. Alex with Chioma?

Was he really going to date her?

I was so mad, instead of the deep, dark, boiling rage, all I could feel was a headache, a thin, reedy pain in the side of my head that made me wince whenever I opened my mouth to talk.

Simon drove me home in silence after I told him I wasn't feeling too fine. He offered to buy me medicine, but I refused.

Why are you hurt? I kept asking myself. It's not like you should be too surprised. I mean, you guys are not dating or anything.

Yeah, but what about the kiss?

The near-kiss had been a mistake, an illusion. Maybe he had just been trying to be friendly, to jolt my memory. Maybe the explosive, Earth-shaking love thing was all in my head. If he felt the same way, he wouldn't be taking Chioma home in front of the whole church. It was like announcing their engagement.

But Simon takes you home all the time, in front of the entire church.

True. Had I inadvertently told everybody I was dating Simon? What if everyone assumed I was with Simon?

How could I not see what's right in front of me?

Damn! Damn! Damn!

Now, Alex was doing the same thing. Tongues would be wagging by now. Chioma and Alex. The thought roiled all night.

That night, I saw Alex in a tuxedo in church watching me as I walked down the aisle to him. But, in the usual manner of dreams, when I got to the aisle and held his hands, my face changed to Chioma.

I woke up panicked, a dark cloud of anger and depression hovering over me.

CHAPTER THIRTEEN

I'm so upset right now. Freaking mad. Just so you know, I am using some curse words that would make you so ashamed of me. And no, this time, it's not about Alex. It's my dad. Yes. My seemingly absent-minded, clueless dad. How could someone so intelligent could totally muck up so much with one thoughtless sentence? You'd think with all the books he reads, he'd at least have a clue into the workings of a woman's mind.

You know, that's my problem with some Nigerian men. They know nothing, absolutely nothing, about women. And they never bother to try to find out. You know why? Because to them, one woman is as good as the other. Yes, I am dissing some Nigerian men, but it's not my fault. The way they treat women is appalling, and in fact, there was a time all I wanted was to date and marry white men. I love the way some of them treasure their women.

God! I'm digressing again. Back to my dad. Let me start from the beginning.

That morning, I prepared pepper soup while Jaja bought soft drinks from a supermarket nearby. My dad hired some plastic chairs from a vendor in my street and arranged them in the family hall. Yes, we have a family hall. Did I mention my dad is the first son in a family of eight kids?

So imagine the vast number of cousins I have. They started arriving pretty early, but still, some came so late, the meeting started by eleven instead of nine.

Nene and her mum were the last to come. I went in to call my mom who had not ventured out of her room since morning. It seems she knew beforehand it would be a disaster.

Just so you know, my mom is not paranoid. I noticed the tight smiles my dad's sisters gave her, the way my cousins cleared their throats and averted their eyes. Clearly, they'd had their own meeting, and my mom had been judged guilty based only on Nene and her mother's testament. I knew then that no matter the outcome, they would not be favourably disposed to my mom. Which is why I pray a lot that when I do get married, my husband's family would love and accept me wholeheartedly.

My dad, being the eldest, started with a prayer, then asked Nene, her mom, and my mom to state their problems with each other.

Nene's mom stated all the perceived slights my mom had inflicted on her since she'd married my dad. She even went back to my mom's wedding day when my mom picked her own sister, Aunt Dorcas, over her to pick up the money guests showered on them when they were dancing. Nene began by stating how she was the last to eat in the house, and how Mom gave her all the housework and shouted at her unnecessarily most times.

When it was my mom's turn, she calmly stated she had nothing to say and sat down. I could tell by the glint in her eyes she was angry.

I was laughing inside. I know my mom hates these meetings, but she should be used to them by now. My dad takes his role as head of the family seriously. He always calls these meetings, sometimes to reprimand bad behaviour, settle issues, and celebrate huge achievements.

As he began his round off speech, I hardly paid attention. My favourite cousin Rico was texting me funny emojis of how he was so weary of these meetings, and I was trying so hard not to laugh.

And then, my dad did the unthinkable. This is the part of the speech I paid attention to:

"... and so, my family, this family must stay together no matter what. I can divorce my wife, but I can never divorce my family."

You see what I mean, right?

How could he say that?

I saw the surprised hurt in my mom's eyes as she stood up and entered her room.

The men laughed, but some of the women looked at my dad disapprovingly. Even though they were not on great terms with my mom, they knew.

Maybe you don't understand, so let me try to explain it.

It's like the girl code, you know, like how you always support your best friend and help her get the guy she likes.

What my dad had done was, to us women, a betrayal. He is expected to stick by his wife, to always support her in public, and gently correct her in private. How could he belittle their marriage in front of his family by saying he could divorce her anytime but not his family?

I mean, maybe Mom has been right all along. His absent-mindedness has definitely been the reason his sisters have never liked my mom. He has never stood up for her.

The meeting rounded up immediately after the disastrous speech. Jaja helped me share the pepper soup, and soon, everyone had dispersed.

By the time I finished cleaning up, it was time for my rehearsals, and Simon was already waiting.

I knew there would be trouble, and sure enough, my mom's door was locked. This was going to be a huge fight. She never locks her door.

Already, I was thinking of ways to settle their issue before it blew out of proportion. And of course, it didn't help Alex was in church during the rehearsals. His car was parked, so he must be in his dad's office.

By the time we finished and came out to leave, he was waiting outside, and Chioma ran to hug him.

I squelched the pain in my heart and grimly sat in the car as Simon drove me home. He also seemed preoccupied as he remained silent 'til he'd dropped me off.

Remember when I said my dad goofed? The proof was in the car I saw parked in the compound and the assailing scent of highly expensive designer perfume that I trailed to my mother's room before I saw her. Aunt Dorcas, my mom's elder sister.

My Aunt Dorcas is a super-rich, super-famous business woman and lawyer who has never been married. Her area of expertise? Divorce.

She's the biggest divorce lawyer in the country. You see all those celebrity and high-profile divorces? She handles most of them and gets paid excellently.

And if her portfolio was not enough to scare you, her appearance would. Aunt Dorcas is tall and big-boned. Her short hair laced with grey is always neatly shining and up kept, as well as her beautiful face which hardly breaks out in smile.

I saw Jaja standing by the door to Mom's room.

"Glory ... How are you?" Aunt Dorcas called out as I attempt to sneak past.

She pulled me into a tight, warm embrace, and I stared at my mom, looking down at the tiles sightlessly.

Diary of a Wallflower

Obviously, Aunt Dorcas had told her a lot to get her thinking.

Suddenly, she smirked and shook her legs in agitation.

"After all these years, he still disrespects me in front of his family. He has never stood up for me. He allows his sisters to talk to me anyhow, even their children have taken to it. And all he can do is to call for a family meeting where he informs them he can divorce me, that he will pick them over me anytime."

Aunt Dorcas laughed bitterly. "You can't trust men to do anything for you, especially stand up for you in front of their family. A woman is just there to make their lives more convenient. You gave up your career for that man. You've given him children. You cook, clean, and basically do everything, and what does he repay you with? Divorce, in front of his family. And this nation does not favour divorced women. Yes. If he divorces you, where will you live? How will you earn a living? Eh? You will end up homeless and broke because you allowed a man be your financial shelter." She shook her head wryly. "And you had a good job. Who knows where you would be if you hadn't quit because of him?"

My mom's lips thinned, and I knew Aunt Dorcas' words had struck home.

"He didn't say he wants to divorce you or anything," I chirped in.

Aunt Dorcas laughed wildly. "Glory, don't be naive. If he's talking about it, he's thinking it, it's an option for him. After all, as a man thinketh in his heart, so he is. Don't ever make this mistake. Don't let a man be the sole breadwinner, else you may end up with nothing. I know thousands and thousands of stories like this. The woman will be a full-time housewife, and the man will kick her out for someone younger. Then, in her old age, she will start suffering and looking for a way to survive and feed her kids."

I gulped because she said the truth. One of the pharmacy shops around is run by a woman whose husband abandoned her and their three kids for someone younger.

I waited patiently for her to leave, then I faced my mom.

"How could you call Aunt Dorcas? You know how she'll start talking about divorce."

My mom turned to me. "You will not understand."

She stood up suddenly and went to the parlour where my dad was sitting, watching the news. And closed the door in our faces.

I smiled at Jaja. We knew they would resolve it in there.

But sadly, we were mistaken.

Because the next thing we heard were angry words. At first, we didn't respond because it was too strange to imagine it would be our parents. They never raise their voices at each other. I mean, it has never been done before.

Then, the door burst open, and Mom whirled out, followed by my dad, the familiar bewildered look on his face.

"You never know anything..." my mom was saying. "So that is really the way you see me, right? I'm just a wife abi, a wife you can divorce anytime. And in front of your family, too? How could you shame me like so?"

My dad looked at me, confused. I shook my head sadly, telling him I wouldn't interfere or help. I'd learnt long before now never to interfere in their issues. Besides, I was a bit angry at not just my dad and Alex but men in general. See how thoughtless they can be. I mean, talking about Alex, he overlooked the multitude of other girls in church, in Port Harcourt, in Nigeria at large, and went for Chioma, my friend. How rude and insensitive could he get?

At the moment, my dad is at a loss for words. Frankly, I don't think he has ever seen my mom so angry.

"I gave you children, I cook and wash for you, I organise your house and have been a companion to you for thirty-three years, Kelechi," Mom continued, obviously in a rage.

My dad winced. Truthfully, my mom has never called him by his name before. Now, he knew she meant business.

"I keep track of all your disorganised files and papers. I left my lucrative job and career, just so you could concentrate on work while I focus on the family, because I thought we were partners. Partners, Kelechi, not just a wife you can divorce at any time as you have so casually announced to your family so they can continue to disrespect me, just like you have been doing all these years. Do you think you are smarter than I am?"

My dad stood, perplexed.

"Tochi, I was just ... just trying to make a point. I didn't mean I want to divorce you."

"You have never defended me or stood up for me in front of your family. Never. I know how I fought my parents to let me marry you then, because you were just a Lecturer's Assistant. But you would never do the same for me."

I could tell my mom was not just speaking from today's incident. This was years and years of anger. Her shoulders hunched as one defeated.

Then, my dad did the worst thing any man can do when a black woman is raking up a storm.

He laughed.

He had the gall to laugh and pat her arm as if talking to an irrational child.

"Don't be irrational, Tochi. I was just trying to make peace."

So my mom glared at him, stalked into her room, and banged the door shut.

For the first time ever, my mom didn't sleep in my dad's room.

CHAPTER FOURTEEN

So, I've been too busy being the mom of the house because the mom of the house is so upset with the dad of the house, she has refused to do her momly/wifely chores, which include cooking and taking care of Jaja.

After I came back from work and saw my dad eating sandwiches at night, I took pity on him.

Seriously, my dad is one of those men who only knows how to boil water. Close as my parents are, or used to be, my dad is so hopeless in the kitchen, even using the toaster was a struggle.

Of course, I had to bribe Jaja with money so he would clean up the house before going to school and I'd have enough time to prepare breakfast for him and Dad.

Frankly, I don't like the turn of events. I didn't know my mom could hold a grudge against my dad for even a day. The situation was only going to get worse, and I knew someone would have to bend over for peace. Obviously, my dad would have to apologise.

But, something terribly exciting happened, and I can't wait to tell you.

It seemed like a normal day of being mom in the house and avoiding Alex like the plague at the office, but all that changed.

I drove to work that day, sitting quietly and sorting out the files on my desk. I didn't even leave for lunch, just worked through 'til everyone had left for the day. I don't know where the energy came from. Maybe all the rage I was feeling had been put to good use.

I was just rounding up with the two last forms on my table when I heard a door close somewhere in the office. I thought I was the only one working late. I didn't even look up at the approaching footsteps until my door opened.

Alex.

At first, my heart leaped, then I remembered Chioma getting into his car. I frowned and looked back to my computer screen.

He approached until he was standing in front of my table.

"Glory."

I ignored him and continued typing blindly, adding a frown to seem more busy.

"Glory," he called again.

Still, I said nothing, just kept on looking at my computer screen.

"Are you going to pretend I'm not here?"

I laughed and said nothing. If my heart was beating fast, again, I took no notice.

He took a deep breath and leaned on my table, relaxing his thighs and setting down his briefcase.

Why wasn't he leaving? I was certain Chioma would be waiting somewhere.

When he spoke again, his voice was gentle and calm. "How are you?"

"Fine," I snapped, tapping away at my keyboard with killer strength.

"I'm sorry," he said softly, again.

"Why? Why are you apologising?" If I wore glasses, I would have removed them and peered at him with a scholarly intimidating look. I made do with crossing my hands underneath my chin and peering at him with hooded eyes.

"Whatever I did that's upset you. I just want us to be friends."

"We're friends."

"Yet, you've been avoiding me, a lot. You even went into the men's room once," he said with a small smile.

"Ouch. You saw it?"

He nodded and smiled, a boyish smile taking me back to the day we sat together in the classroom block.

"I'm not crazy, I tell you ..."

He laughed, hard ... and the unease disappeared. Then, we talked, about everything that had happened since we'd left school. I told him Mabel had married that Frank guy even before she'd gained admission into university. He told me how he had received a job offer in Ukraine which he'd declined because of his parents' insistence he return home. I get the feeling Pastor Lanre wanted his elder son to succeed him, but I kept quiet.

It wouldn't be a bad idea for Alex to be the next senior pastor. Already, the church flocked to his side, and everyone had nice words to say about him. He would make an excellent heads man.

Of course, I drifted off in my head, and he had to call my name several times to get my attention back to him.

You see, I'm wired differently than others. You may think it abnormal to have conversations in your head, but not me. I talk to myself in my head a lot, and I don't regard it as strange. Years of being friendless had taught me that, and I was a good student.

Of course, it was perfectly normal when he walked me to my car and leaned in for a goodnight hug.

Then, things went to the other side, or as Buhari would put it, the other room.

He didn't know I was melting inside, being held in his arms, however brief. And I couldn't blame him for leaning in to whisper goodnight into my ear. Now that was the big mistake.

My ears are really sensitive, and his words sent a special shiver down my spine.

Just as I turned my head to say goodnight, he turned to look at me. Our lips brushed across each other's.

I have been kissed before yes, but you see, Alex has the softest lips in the entire world, and I'm not exaggerating. They're softer than a baby's lips. How he does it, I don't know, but we did kiss, for a long time.

I didn't want it to end. I don't know who finally pulled apart, but I stood there, looking into his eyes until the flashing light of a head lamp from a passing car buried us in bright white light.

I hurriedly entered my car and drove off, hoping my lips would stop trembling by morning. My heart kept thumping and singing 'he kissed me' over and over again.

Okay. I know the kiss was an accident, but he wouldn't have continued if he hadn't wanted to. Which meant, there was no way he was dating Chioma. Maybe I was just being paranoid. After all, I only saw her getting into his car. She was the one who ran to hug him, not the other way round. What else could he do but hug her back? It would have being rude not to. I can't jump to such huge conclusions.

I was still smiling when I got home and realised the Cold War continued there. Mom's door was shut tight, and Dad was staring listless at the television.

I had to do something. I couldn't just sit back and watch this, right?

I sat beside Dad, and he smiled sadly at me.

"How was work?"

"It was fine. About Mom ..."

He laughed wryly. "We'll resolve it. Your mom is just being stubborn."

I laughed. "And Aunt Dorcas is not helping matters."

"Your aunt is ... well, she had a bitter experience, and it has coloured the way she sees everything."

The door burst open, and Mom whirled in, eyes blazing, and stuck her phone in Dad's face. "Who is this girl, Kelechi? Is this the reason you want to divorce me?"

It was a picture of Dad with a young girl, probably one of his students, beside his car, in front of Genesis restaurant.

He just stared at it. "How did you ... are you now following me?"

"Answer the question. Who is she?"

Dad stood up, clearly upset. "When did you start losing trust in me? Your sister is putting nonsense ideas into your head."

"No, she's not. And don't talk about Dorcas like that. Now explain who this woman is."

Dad shook his head and walked away.

I stood, immobile as she sat down heavily.

"Your father is cheating on me with one of his students."

I didn't have a word to say to her. "Did you follow him?"

"No. Dorcas sent it to me just now. I have always trusted your father. Always. Is this what I get? After thirty-three years."

Their fight almost weighed me down, but I wasn't surprised when the next morning, my lips were still trembling, and I couldn't quite look into Alex's eyes in the office.

I kept waiting for the closing hour, watching the clock tick away. Juliet, who by this time, had given up on her pursuit of Alex by going back to moderate skirts, kept asking why I was glancing at the wall clock every now and then.

I smiled to myself, and she grinned. Luckily, she didn't pursue it further, although I felt she must have had an idea. I mean, she must definitely have noticed how I'd get all clumsy and high-pitched whenever Alex came around. I was grateful she hadn't said anything just yet, maybe gathering enough evidence before stating her claims.

All I wanted was to be in his arms again. After office hours, I'd run and hug him, and maybe we'd kiss again.

I kept looking to his door, hoping to catch a glimpse of him. So it wasn't really an accident when I saw Chioma walk into his office. And it only seemed natural for him to rise and hug her just before the door shut. The smile froze on my face.

There are storms, then there are tempests. I remember a tale from *Lamb Tales from Shakespeare* I had read in my Junior Secondary. The very first tale had described a fiery tempest that led to complications, one of such being of the romantic kind.

But I wasn't dwelling on anything romantic. No. What I felt was anger, a deep-seated anger swirling like a rapidly burning pot of ogbonno soup.

I burned with rage, barely containing myself with mutterings and deep scowls that kept Georgewill and Juliet at bay the rest of the day, even after Chioma had left, escorted by the two-timing gentleman, no less. They didn't even say goodnight to me as they left.

I've been angry before, but it had always been a controlled one. The least I'd do would be to ball my fists and try to keep myself in check. I'm very lithe and thin. There are some winds that could actually lift me up and carry me away, so I learnt rather young how my power lies not in physical strength.

But I forgot all of it as Alex approached me as I closed my office door. I thought he had left with Chioma. What galled was how he had the effrontery to smile the sweet deceptive smile of his that always worked magic.

Well, today, it didn't work its magic. Or it worked a different kind of magic that made me wait 'til he came in for a hug before I slapped him.

Yeah, I did slap him.

Was I wrong?

As you can guess, diary, I was conflicted about my actions. I mean, he did deserve it—after all, why was he being all hanky-panky with Chioma, right after being all kissy-smoochy with me? He's a two-timing man. He did the same with Miriam in school. Only problem is, in this case, I'm Miriam, and Chioma is me. You understand the logic, right?

But then again, it's not right to slap a man. I felt like I had just desecrated a most sacrilegious object, being the male species. Pastor Lanre has often drummed it into our ears, "Young ladies, when you get married, don't get physical with your husband or any man ... The minute you do that, he sees you being confrontational, and he'll never back down. He's a man, he's built to be confrontational. Instead, use your feminine wiles ..."

I could almost see the look of disappointment in Pastor Lanre's eyes, and I groaned. How could I explain this one?

I know Simon would not even agree with me on this. Damn. I should have held my anger in check. I mean, he was only talking to her; it's not like he has given her a ring or anything.

But he took her home. He's obviously interested. And then, she came to visit him in his office, no less. There's something there.

You know what? I'm totally right. There's definitely something there.

And if there was, I had just pushed him completely into her arms. Ahhhhhh!

I should have played it cool, embraced him, and treated him nice. I mean, I know these things in my head, but acting it out becomes a problem.

You know how you can solve all your friends' relationship issues, but you're totally clueless when it comes to yours? Yup. That's me.

I know antagonism and nagging are the surest ways of driving a man into another woman's arms. Yet, here I am, guilty of said practice.

The only explanation I have is, when it comes to Alex, I lose all rational reasoning.

I have always condemned women who seemingly go all weak and helpless at the sight of a man they have feelings for. 'Be rational,' I'd advise them hotly, 'Can't you see you're doing the wrong thing?'

Even now, I know the rational thing to do would be to apologise, but, of course, my legs would always run in the opposite direction whenever I saw him coming. And that was only in the office, during briefings or meetings or work-related issues.

He didn't seek me out, and I didn't seek him out. He would just look through me like I'm invisible every time we happened upon each other by accident.

I know you're thinking I'm proud. It's easy for you to say. Have you ever felt so awkward, so tongue-twisted, you know you'd just babble and make a fool of yourself in front of somebody you're trying to be all cool and casual with?

Besides, who said he'd accept my apology? I'd given him the biggest insult a girl could give to a man. I'm sure I would be listed number one in his black book.

So yeah, what's the point of even trying?

It's not like he's making any effort to talk to me. Nah. He's too busy, using every available opportunity with Chioma.

So when I got to rehearsals on Saturday and saw them laughing together, of course, my face immediately became hard. I faked a smile and took my seat.

Then, the man-stealer herself, Chioma, came to sit beside me, still grinning from what must have been a romantic conversation.

"Oh, Alex is so funny ..." she said as she wiped her brow with a handkerchief.

I grunted and shifted to give her more room.

"I came to your office on Monday. I didn't see you," she said so off-handedly that I immediately took offence.

"You didn't come to see me, so ..." I was looking into my phone screen, waiting to hear what she'd say next, what excuse she'd give for being at Alex's office.

She didn't say anything, just looked at me strangely and grunted.

Gosh. I know I'm being a terrible Christian right now. With all this bad attitude, jealousy, envy, malice, anxiety, and lust, how could I even call myself a Christian again? I felt ashamed.

Lord, I try. I really do, but sometimes, these things just get to me. How do I stop being so angry, and jealous, and vain? How do I give up this lust?

I didn't get any reply, not even the small voice that whispers in my heart and comforts me. My attitude had kept the Holy Spirit quiet. How far would I stray from God just because of unrequited love?

I stood up and went to my spot as I call it beside the generator house. Always lonely and loud, nobody ventured here. I got on my knees and began to sing. I sang 'til I felt it, the peace only the presence of God can give. I wiped the tears from my eyes and stood up, cleaning my knees.

Somebody coughed. I jerked my head up to look at Simon. He smiled at me, and I smiled back and ran into his arms. It wasn't strange, him seeing me here. It was our spot. The one place we'd hang out in and pray secretly without any interference.

"Do you want to talk about it?" he asked.

I shook my head and wiped my face with his shirt.

"Let's go."

We went back to the choir stand, and I took my seat. Subconsciously, I glanced towards Alex. He sat with several men, having a discussion in the far right wing of the church. Strange, I felt like he was watching me.

I kept having this feeling all through rehearsals, even though every time I looked, he seemed deep in conversation. Then, I remembered. Chioma was sitting next to me. If he had been looking, it definitely hadn't been directed at me. The old jealousy wanted to creep up. I held my breath and calmed my heartbeat. I wouldn't let jealousy interfere with my relationship with God again.

Standing beside Simon's car, I was scrolling through Facebook when Simon and Chioma walked to me. Of course, Alex was with them, and definitely, Chioma was laughing gaily and holding unto his arm. Since when did Alex become a comedian?

"Glory," Chioma called out as she came to me. "Can you believe Alex has never been to Lumières?"

"No. I can't believe it."

"Yes. We're going there tomorrow."

Of course they were. Alex and Chioma having dinner at the most romantic restaurant in town; there was nothing wrong with that picture.

"What's the big deal about Lumières?" Alex directed his question to Simon who grinned and shrugged.

"It's the place chicks are crazy about now."

"Oh."

Was I the only one feeling the tension? I had slapped him just days ago, a day after the sweetest kiss I'd ever had. He was standing so close, and the evening breeze brought his cologne to my nose. Oh, God ... I wanted to be the one holding his hands, laughing and looking into his face, standing next to him. Oh, no, the feelings were back. He was probably despising me because of the slap, and here I was, dying to hold his hands.

"So you ever been there?" Alex asked Simon.

"Yes. Once."

"Really? With who?"

I squirmed as Simon called my name. I suddenly found the interlocked tiles on the ground much more interesting than the conversation going on around me.

Alex grunted. "That means you both know what's good on the menu. Maybe we should all go together."

I held my breath as Simon said yes and shook hands with him. Simon and I together with Chioma and Alex. In his mind, he thought he was arranging a double date. What he didn't know was that Simon was not my boyfriend. I shook my head with anger. This was going to be torture. The date was set for Sunday evening. I shrugged and nodded as Simon asked if I'd be free. Chioma was positively radiating with joy.

"Are you okay?" Simon asked.

"Yes ..." I cleared my throat. "Yes, I'm fine."

"So, has she told you I'm ready to do the Kierra Sheard song?" Chioma asked Simon. They went into the building, looking for Ifeanyi, the keyboardist.

I was left standing with Alex. I could feel his gaze on me.

"Are you really so proud?"

My head whipped up. "What?"

"You can't apologise for slapping me? Instead, you'd avoid me like the plague."

Where did he get off sounding so bossy? Was he right for kissing me and dating Chioma at the same time?

I ground my teeth and looked away stubbornly.

"Ah! The silent treatment." He moved closer until he was leaning on the car, so close to me. "I know why you did it. You were angry ... because of the ... the ..."

"The kiss?" I asked bluntly, looking straight in his face. Was he ashamed of the kiss?

"Yes. I realize I deserved that slap. I feel very ... ashamed. I shouldn't have done it."

Every word was like a piercing pain in my heart. He was ashamed of kissing me?

"I mean, you're with—" He stopped mid-sentence as Simon came back with Chioma.

As expected, he drove her home.

Thanks to my prayer in church, I asked the Holy Spirit to help me deal with the lust and the grace to stop loving Alex and let him be with the woman of his choice. It was the perfect choice.

But how are you sure you're not the woman of his choice?

I know the voice asking this question. It seems like a rational and logical part of me, but it always leaves me double-minded. This time, I won't be deceived. If Alex wanted me, he wouldn't be dating Chioma. I must believe this pain will fade away with time, and when I meet the right one, I'll be ready and free to love him. I have to let go of Alex. It's the only rational thing to do. For my peace of mind.

CHAPTER FIFTEEN

Sunday evening arrived with trepidation and a hint of excitement. I placed the excitement on the good food I would eat at Lumières, but the moment my gaze landed on Alex, I knew it wasn't about food.

Have you ever loved someone so deeply, so strongly, so intensely, their presence is intoxicating? He stood handsome as ever in a striped white shirt that illuminated his dark skin. I felt it again—undeniable lust. But not just that. A sweet tenderness, a gentle peace making my heart smile. I had it bad.

You have to understand why Lumières is a chick place. Up until last year, they had been the usual upscale restaurant enjoyed on dates and all until this year's Valentine when fifteen marriage proposals had taken place in its setting. The restaurant had taken advantage of that stroke of luck and termed themselves the Most Romantic Restaurant. Of course, ladies flocked their men into there, hoping a bit of said luck would bring a proposal.

Chioma was definitely angling for something here. What if the magic of Lumières made them fall in love even more? Would Alex propose to her here, in front of me? I don't drink alcohol, but suddenly, I needed a good dose of strong spirit to stomach the evening.

Lumières is a beautiful place, set with the most romantic colours and an intimate setting that all but shoved love right into your face. It was like a world made just for lovers. My heart skipped as we stepped into the luscious foyer and Simon led us to a booth for four.

By a twist of fate, Alex slid into the booth right after I sat down. I wanted to protest. Why was he sitting next to me? He should be sitting with his date. Maybe he was sitting opposite her so he could look into her eyes whenever he wanted.

I picked up my menu and left the conversation to them. It was pure torture, to have him so close and yet so far. I gripped my hands together to stop my hands from touching his arm, from brushing across his elbow. *Look at me. Love me.*

I felt his light touch on my arm before I realized they had asked me a question. Of course, I stuttered an unintelligible answer to an obscure question and went back to heartbroken silence. Every time his arm touched Chioma, my heart would skip a beat. Every time he smiled at her, my heart would sky-rocket, and every time he held her hand and paid attention to her, my sky-rocketing heart would plunge nose-down to the ground.

What does one need when dining with an ex they still love but who's with somebody else?

Alcohol.

Unfortunately, I couldn't have any. It's been five years since I touched alcohol, not that I was much of a drinker before then. I just took the little drinks made for girls and stayed within a limit of two glasses.

I remember the first night I took alcohol. I never touched it 'til I got into university. At a time when exams were over and we were pretty low on cash, I met a family friend, an overweight man, who offered to take me out. Of course, two of my friends tagged along on a day of snacks, good food, haircut, and car rides. It ended with a visit to a club.

Shy, I watched my friends dance away gaily. I couldn't imagine standing up to dance in a room full of strangers. I mean, I felt like they would all just start laughing at me. But I knew I was a good dancer. I decided alcohol would loosen me up. Innocently, I began to gulp down whatever was placed in front of me and ended up barfing all over my uncle's newly washed car all night. We left so late, he took us to his hotel to spend the night, thoughtfully placing a bucket beside me, which I barfed into occasionally. The next morning, I had such a hangover, I decided never to overstep my bounds.

I felt a light touch in my arm, and startled. Alex.

"Where have you been?"

All three were staring at me with big eyes full of questions. I was being weird, and even I knew it. In that moment, while they all stared at me, I made up my mind. I decided to be mature about this and move on. I decided to stop throwing pity parties in my head and start living in the moment. Here I am, blessed with a great family, great friends, great church, great job, great life, sitting at Lumières, and still, I found a way to be unhappy. Was I addicted to unhappiness, to a feeling of inadequacy or never being enough?

No—I made up my mind.

So I laughed gaily and smiled warmly at Simon.

"Yes. I was remembering the first time I got drunk."

Simon roared with laughter.

"What about it? What's so funny?" Alex asked, his interest piqued.

"Glory threw up all over her uncle's newly washed car. She kept on puking all night and ended up dancing in the hotel lobby."

"You went to a hotel with your uncle?" Alex asked, a frown on his face.

"No. He took me and my friends out."

"Oh!"

Chioma laughed gaily. "That's why I've decided never to touch alcohol again. Right, Alex?"

He nodded and drank from his glass. I watched his throat bob up and down, then looked away, right at Simon watching me with a queer look in his eyes. Oh, no. Had he seen me staring at Alex?

Maybe he'd guess Alex was the guy I'd been talking to him about the other day. I suddenly found my food very interesting. Then, my leg accidentally brushed against Alex's underneath the table. I stayed still, then slowly removed my legs and sat up straight.

"Glory, you have something in your ... wait, let me remove it." Simon leaned forward over the table and removed whatever was stuck on my lips.

I could feel the heat radiating from Alex, hot and intense. Surreptitiously, I glanced at him sideways and noticed the way he gripped his cutlery tightly. Was he jealous?

If he was jealous, it meant he cared.

The joy was just beginning to radiate in my heart, then he held Chioma's hand and began to speak to her in a quiet voice. False alarm, *heart*.

I could just imagine my heart, arms crossed and stamping her foot at me. I must have given her so many false alarms these past weeks.

Simon left to re-park his car. I left Alex to have his quiet loving conversation with Chioma. It's like they were in their own world, oblivious to my hurting presence.

After toying with my phone awkwardly for a while, I concentrated on the music channel in the TVs placed strategically all around the restaurant.

How rude for the two of them to ignore me completely. This was the last time I'd ever go out with Alex or Chioma. I mean, this was supposed to be a 'double date.' The least they could do was involve me in their conversation. Jerks, acting like they were the first persons to ever fall in love.

Fine. If they could ignore me so bad, I'd do the same to them. The music channel kept me entertained, with the images of near-naked girls and flashy cars. Damn. It was a world of illusion up there. Is this really what people call entertainment? Nobody sings a song without showing off a bevy of naked ladies. Not even the female artists. How could they allow themselves to be used in such a manner? Then again, I can't be a judge over them.

I felt a light touch on my hands and looked up at Alex. Where was Chioma?

"You still do this," he said, still holding my hand.

"Do what?"

"Drifting off into your own world."

"You two were busy, having a private conversation. So, no, I wasn't drifting," I replied saucily.

He held my arm and kept staring at me in a way that left me hot and bothered. Where was Chioma? And just how long did it take to re-park a car? Simon had been gone for more than twenty minutes.

"What are you thinking of?" Alex asked, still holding my arm.

Had he forgotten to remove it? It was burning into my skin.

"Nothing." I shuffled uncomfortably, thankful he couldn't read my thoughts. How shameful would that be?

He just kept staring at me, with a look I couldn't recognise, making me feel like a lab snake under scrutiny, under intense observation by zealous scientists about to undergo a risky new experiment.

"I'm just wondering what's taking Simon so long?"

Abruptly, he scuttled towards me, relaxing his back on the booth and circling rings on my palm. I struggled not to shiver.

"Why? Are you uncomfortable being alone with me?"

I nodded furiously and tried to drag my hand away. He only tightened his grip and smiled radiantly at me, like he knew what effect his touch has on me. He couldn't possibly ...

"Why do you keep running?"

I pretended ignorance. "Running?"

"You know what I mean. You keep avoiding me. We used to be really good friends ... why can't we be that anymore?"

Friends? Was this how he remembered our relationship in the past?

"We were more than friends, Alex."

"I thought you didn't remember that part."

No. Everything was burned into my brain.

"I still remember our first kiss ..." He edged closer.

I scuttled farther into the booth. Distance. I needed distance.

"I still remember that night ... like it was yesterday," he continued, his eyes burning into mine.

I felt my body lean closer, drawn like a moth to Alex's flame.

I cleared my throat and looked around wildly. Chioma. Where had she disappeared to?

"We were so young ..." he said, his breath so close.

"And foolish," I threw in.

"Do you think everything we had then was a result of adolescent foolishness? Is that how you—forget it."

He dropped my hand and moved away from me. What had I said to make him so angry?

Surely, he'd realise I was only playing down things to make him more comfortable, so he wouldn't realise that I was stuck in the past.

"I haven't forgotten that night, either," I said quietly, as Simon and Chioma came back in and sat down breezily.

"Sorry. I met an old friend outside," Simon apologised.

Company, at last.

"Alex ..." Chioma called out. "How long have you been in Ukraine?"

"Eight years," I replied automatically.

The noise died down, and I looked up slowly. Everyone was looking at me strangely.

"Yes. Eight years ..." Alex said, with a look of interest in his eyes.

"Wait." Chioma had a glint in her eyes I could only call calculating. "How did you know?"

I shuffled into my seat. How would I get out of this one?

Be mature, Glory. It's not a big deal if people know you two attended the same high school. It's not an engagement announcement.

"We attended the same high school," Alex said and shrugged non-committally, like it was not a big deal.

Which it wasn't. It definitely wasn't a big deal.

Simon and Chioma looked on in surprise.

"You didn't tell me," Simon directed at me, a look in his eyes.

I knew he was putting two and two together, realising Alex was the ex-boyfriend I had been talking about earlier.

Gosh! Now he would pity me. Crushing on an ex who was dating a friend.

I started avoiding Simon's eyes the rest of the night. No mean feat. He didn't let me rest, either, kept on prodding and prodding.

"So, were you two friends back in high school?" Simon asked casually.

I grinned nervously and stuffed my mouth with delicious basmati rice. Let Alex handle *that* one.

He grinned ... then held my hand in a loving gesture.

"We were more than friends, Simon."

"What?" Chioma shrieked. "You mean you two ... actually dated?"

She had this look of strong disbelief in her eyes, like she couldn't comprehend it. I was annoyed.

"Yes," I replied strongly. "We were high school sweethearts. We even won an award for being the best couple of the year."

I grinned beautifully at her. What did she think, that Alex was too good for me? No. In fact, I was the one too good for Alex.

"But you two are hardly friends now ..." Simon poked in.

I shrugged. It wasn't my fault my stubborn heart put me in a position where I had to evade any promise of friendship with Alex.

Alex smiled and concentrated on his meal.

"Why?" Simon asked.

We looked up, surprised.

"Why what?" Alex quipped.

"Why are you two not friends anymore? And why did you break up in the first place?"

Why wouldn't he let it rest? I took a big sip of my Chapman and left Alex to handle *another* one.

"We never actually ... officially broke up. It was more of a distance thing"

Funny. We never officially broke up.

Simon smiled mischievously, and I knew he was about to say something ... outlandish.

"So that means you two ... are still unofficially together," he crooned.

And I was right.

Chioma laughed awkwardly. I could tell she was a bit uncomfortable. Maybe if she had known our history, she wouldn't have invited me to this dinner. Then again, she hadn't invited me. Alex had.

I kicked Simon underneath the table, causing him to spill a little of his drink on his shirt. The jerk. He'd only brought this up to make me uncomfortable. He hadn't considered Chioma. I had to put her mind at ease.

"Simon, don't be ridiculous. It all happened long ago. We were basically teenagers. Time and adulthood have put an end to all that."

Alex grinned and downed his drink. His nails were clipped and cut short. He had long fingers, slim and bony, which would seem feminine on any other man, but on Alex, only made him more assured.

I looked at my long nails and hid them under the table.

Chioma smiled at me in appreciation.

"Besides, everyone had a teenage romance fling in secondary school. It's not the stuff love stories are made of," I continued, spurred on by the smile now on Chioma's face. Good. She wasn't so shaky.

Maybe, when I get used to seeing them together, these feelings would fade away. It was for the best, anyways—the emotions I felt now were too wild, too volatile to be the real thing. Love, the true love that endures and keeps people together until old age, cannot surely be this whirlwind of feelings and emotions, lust, and whacky insomnia. No. Love should be peaceful, a quiet and steady assurance like a rock. All these intense feelings were just left-over memories from my adolescent years.

Yeah. Hope you feel the same way when you get an invite to their wedding.

Ha. Before that ever happens, I'd be well and truly over Alex.

And pigs can fly.

Alex suddenly looked right at me, as if he had just decided to speak up, to correct an impression.

"I think it's wrong to try to discount what we had as purely raging teenage hormones. Some great love stories have been known to begin from childhood. Besides, what I felt for you at the time wasn't just hormones."

Alex.

Why was he making it seem like an epic love tale? Couldn't he see his *new* girlfriend was uncomfortable?

"And besides ..." he continued. "There is something wildly sweet and innocent in tender aged love. Maybe at the time, you were motivated by hormones. I wasn't."

Why was he sounding bitter? I turned to face him squarely. "What are you talking about?"

He faced me, too, a hard glint in his eyes. "That falling in love for the first time, especially at a young age, is *not* the flippant, depthless thing you're trying to make it seem."

I scoffed. "Why? Teenagers who *claim* to be in love are only suffering from exaggerated hormone-induced feelings that have no basis. Teenage boys are more concerned with scoring notches on their bed posts than anything with depth. Love is too difficult a concept to understand at that age."

"But it's not difficult to feel. Glory, I'm not talking about boys trying to prove themselves. I'm talking about those who actually and truly do fall in love at a tender age."

I took a deep breath and shook my head like a patient mother trying to explain life's challenges to her irrational teenage son. "And every woman can testify teenage relationships are two immature brains trying to comprehend something bigger than them. What can two teenagers possibly know about love?"

"When two people truly love each other, they will find a way to make it work. I believe it strongly, and I find it disheartening you don't. The proof is not in words but in how hard you try to make it work, instead of just giving up." Alex was looking straight into my eyes now.

"I didn't just give up. You travelled out, and I never heard from you again."

"I couldn't call, but I sent you thousands of emails, which you never bothered to reply."

"And so? Like you weren't busy with other girls over there ..."

"What are you talking about?" he all but roared in my face.

"Oh, don't pretend like you don't know what I'm talking about. Your Facebook posts ..."

"What posts?"

Damn. Now he would know I had stalked him on Facebook. Pathetic.

I took a sip of my drink. "It doesn't matter, Alex. It was a teenage romance that didn't mean anything."

"I loved you."

His voice was a whisper, so firm yet soft. I froze with my drink halfway to my mouth.

Damn, Alex. Why now? Why? Just when I'm about getting over you.

He'd loved me. My heart soared, and I smiled a bit ... Until I remembered. Oh, yeah, his new girlfriend was seated right in front of me.

But he'd loved me, and that mattered. It meant it hadn't all been in my head. All those years, I thought I had been the only one in love. He'd loved me right back.

Even now, when it was too late, I realised it was a comfort to know how he'd felt.

I looked away and sipped my drink. The silence at the table was deafening. I could hear the crickets chirping away in the lawn.

Chioma chipped in. "The fault cannot lie at one person's feet. At that age, no one is thinking of forever. Life moves everybody in different directions."

That was when Alex held her hand and smiled. "I know."

Hmmm. The fight had left him. Chioma could calm the anger inside him. What did it make me?

Suddenly, the image of Alex in one of his violent rages in high school popped into my head. I had never managed to calm the wilder part of him.

I bent my head and peered into my phone to hide the tears in my eyes. *Oh, Alex. Why do you still affect me so?*

I knew more tears were on their way. I stood up hurriedly and went into the ladies'.

The way he'd melted because of Chioma, just like Hulk goes down when he sees whatever her name is. Chioma was his calm waters, his peace, which made me his troubled waters, his chaos.

Whatever. Be strong. The night is almost over.

Yes. And I'm never doing this 'double date' thing again. It's hard enough trying to get over Alex while having to see him in work and in church. I didn't have to add social gatherings to the list.

I washed my hands up, dusted light powder on my nose, and left the convenience.

Simon was standing outside when I stepped out. I smiled shakily at him and continued to walk. He held me, forcing me to stop.

"I'm sorry. I didn't know things would get ... like that. I shouldn't have brought it up."

It really wasn't his fault I was still in love with Alex, or that said love object had a new girlfriend, or that he blamed me for the way it ended.

"You don't have to apologise, Simon."

He grinned, and I knew he was back. The devil.

"So, just to clarify, it's him you were talking about the other day, right?"

I gave him the bad eye and continued to walk.

He logged behind and whistled loudly. "Glory's in love with Alex ..."

"I'm not in love with him. Left-over feelings, remember? Besides, why would I be looking for another man when I have you in my life?"

He held up his arms. "Don't use me as an excuse. I know you still have feelings for him. Maybe you even still love him."

"Don't be ridiculous. It was so long ago."

"So long ago, yet, you still carry a torch." Simon whistled and gaily walked past.

Chioma and Alex were ready to leave.

I quickly carried my dainty purse and walked with Simon to the car. He was quiet on the drive home and didn't speak even when he dropped me off.

My mind kept whirling, like a hamster in a wheel, constantly running and creating a perfect circle. I couldn't deny the chemistry between the two of them. I wanted to be happy for them, to let go before jealousy crept up. *Why can't I be happy, Lord?*

Why did he have to pop right back into my life at a time when I feel so ... incomplete?

Great. Now I felt like I was in a terribly romantic movie. You know, those ones that have us girls starry-eyed and sighing happily at the end, a total chick flick. I love chick flicks. They're the only kind of movies I watch, not that I don't appreciate the drama, action, and intriguing blockbusters out there.

But the way I see it, there is already so much tragedy in the world. I mean, watching the news stations is like a trip into discouragement and depression land with all the horrors going on in the world. Why not fill my eyes with happily-ever-after stories?

Anyways, I know it may take a while for me to get over Alex. Again.

He's like a complex Maths equation in an exam. No matter how you try, it can't be avoided. And I have to confront him, head on.

CHAPTER SIXTEEN

I continued avoiding Alex.

Don't laugh at me, diary. I know I said I would confront him, my feelings for him head on. But it's not so easy. What do I say? That I still love him? I'm not even sure it's love, maybe just forgotten hormones trying to rear their heads again.

How do I raise all this dust with him? He's obviously moved on, long ago, if I might say. I can't have him know I'm still stuck on him, living in the past like a ghost. The worst part is, he didn't try to talk to me. Not once.

It is for the best. I'm glad I didn't make a fool of myself before him. He's obviously serious about Chioma. Maybe, just like me, he has let go of his past and moved on.

So why are you not happy?

Ignore the niggling voice in my head. I'm happy.

Okay. I thought I was ... Until Rowland, a guy I work with, asked me out.

That Thursday, I was trying to get into my car to get to evening service. Lately, my door has been giving me issues. It kept getting more difficult to open, and I was just ready to give up on it when Rowland offered to help.

He got the door open, and then, he said the dreaded words. 'Will you go out with me ... on a date?'

His hands were trembling slightly. He was nervous. Before I could say no, Alex walked past. I jumped guiltily, like I had been caught in an embarrassing act. He barely acknowledged us as he got into his car and drove off.

Rowland was still waiting for an answer. What reason did I have to turn him down?

None at all.

I said yes hastily and climbed into my car. The traffic made me arrive late, and I rushed in after the service had begun.

Pastor Lanre began a sermon that seemed aimed at me—Letting go of the past.

How can I move into the future if my whole being is centred and focused on my past? Let go of the 'good old days' and make today count.

I took the message to heart, glad I had accepted Rowland's invite.

The times I'd had with Alex had been great, but I had to look towards my future.

I dressed with care for my date with Rowland the next morning, wearing a black gown that would do for work and an early evening date.

As I parked my car, Rowland walked up to me, smiling.

I smiled back as he approached. He was quite good-looking and had an innocent smile. I knew even if it didn't work out between us, we'd still be friends.

"Hi," he whispered, slightly out of breath.

Or was he just a bit shy? How sweet.

It made me feel free, alive, and beautiful. A man could still be shy over me. I smiled widely.

"Good morning. How was your night?" I asked as I locked my door.

He nodded enthusiastically.

"It was good." He swallowed audibly. "So, we're still on for tonight. Right?"

"Of course."

By a stroke of luck, Alex drove in at the same moment.

I quickly moved into the building, to avoid meeting Alex. Avoiding him, remember?

Rowland went into his department, and I went to my desk. Georgewill and Juliet immediately flanked my side.

Georgewill started. "So ... when were you going to tell us?"

"Tell you what?" I asked, opening my drawer and pulling out my records.

Juliet dragged them from my hands. "Don't pretend."

I looked up at the two of them, standing so close with eager attention.

"Okay. What are you guys talking about?" I leaned down on my seat until they broke the news.

"You and Mr. Alex attended the same school."

"What?" How did they find out?

"The same secondary school, Glory. Don't play dumb," Juliet cautioned.

"How ..." I began.

"Don't worry about the how ... why didn't you tell us?" Georgewill scolded.

They were dead serious.

"Because it's not important."

Juliet gasped. I know. Over-dramatic.

"What are you gasping for? How is it even important that Alex and I attended the same school?"

They exchanged a look. Uh, oh. I know the look. They had found out something.

"What is it?"

They cleared their throats and went back to their seats quickly just as the door opened and Alex strode in. My heart went into over-drive. I had avoided him ever since the 'double date,' ever since he'd said he'd loved me. How could I forget? It was the voice I heard at night, just before I slept. Those words had me tossing and turning, thinking up crazy possibilities. Those words, three letters in the past tense, had put so much hope inside me, I knew if I continued to be close to him, I'd give him my heart all over again.

He already has it.

I ignored the voice and focused on Alex's. He turned to me.

"Bring me the Arthur case files in twenty minutes, Glory," he snapped and left.

I made a face behind him and sat down, huffed.

"You two don't even act like you know each other," Juliet said as she tapped away, her fingers flying over her keyboard without any mistake, I was sure. It was like her ninja skill.

I shrugged and kept my head focused on my screen, not wanting more probing.

I took a deep breath going into his office. We hadn't spoken since that night, since he'd said those damn three words. No. I wouldn't let him see he'd affected me.

His head was bent on his table as I stepped in. He motioned for me to drop the files without looking up.

I dropped them obediently, pleased I didn't have to speak to him, and turned to leave.

He held his hands up, halting my movements. I skipped from leg to leg, frightened that when he'd look up, in his eyes, all I'd see would be those words, and I'd melt.

I waited. And waited. He was still writing furiously on his pad. I cleared my throat to remind him of my presence. He didn't look up, just kept scribbling on his pad.

Then, he motioned me out of his office.

Weird.

Maybe he had also decided putting distance between us would be the wise thing.

Or maybe he is not affected by you at all.

I squelched the cruel voice. After all, I had a date after work. It didn't matter either way, who was affected and who wasn't.

By evening, I removed my jacket, freshened my make-up, and went to my car. Standing beside my car was Alex. I faltered, then concentrated on walking with slow, steady steps.

He didn't say a word, just gave me this look I didn't understand.

"What do you want?" I called irritably.

"What are you doing with Rowland?"

I gasped. "How did you ..."

"That's not important." He waved it away. "Why do you want to cheat on Simon?"

What?

"What are you talking about?"

He grabbed my arm furiously, then quickly dropped it as if scalded, a look of pain or regret in his eyes.

"I'm sorry. I didn't mean to ..." He gestured to my arm.

Why was he acting so torn up about it? Oh, yeah, his violent days in school.

"It's okay, Alex. It didn't hurt. See?" I held out my arm.

He breathed a sigh of relief. It obviously meant a great deal if he'd hurt me.

"After the ... um, terrible way I acted back then in school, I have to be very ... careful. I don't do that anymore. I want you to know. No. I *need* you to know."

"I know, Alex. You don't have to worry."

He nodded curtly, then glanced at my gown. "You haven't answered my question."

I grinned nervously and opened my car. He took my bag and put it in the backseat, as if he had been doing it for a long time.

For just a tiny moment, I allowed myself to imagine we were going home together. His next words snapped me out of my reverie.

"When did you become a cheat?"

I stilled. He didn't take it as a warning—he went on.

"You say you're born again, yet here you are about to cheat on a good man like Simon."

I laughed wickedly as a thousand and one bitter retorts jumped to my lips. *Holy Spirit, help me.*

I took a deep breath and spoke calmly. "I'm not cheating."

"So what are you doing with Rowland?" he persisted.

I shrugged. "Nothing that concerns you."

He looked perplexed. Whatever! He had no right to question me about anything. I had respected his decision and tried my best to stay out of his relationship with Chioma. What right did he have to question me?

I got into my car and went to the restaurant earlier than intended, sipping an orange drink while waiting for Rowland, valiantly trying to calm my raging anger down. I wish I could tell him exactly what I felt and thought. Oh, to be kind-worded can be so hard sometimes.

God, I try. I'm trying.

Growing up, I had been called saucy and accused of having an attitude problem by literally every adult wanting to send me on errands. I think it's malicious when adults tend to do whatever they want to kids and expect them to be silent robots. I mean, they shouldn't have absolute power over kids just because they are older, right?

As a kid, I remember feeling so many intense emotions and wondering why the adults never thought I had anything to say, why they always dismissed my feelings and thoughts as irrelevant. Having a quick retort had been my weapon and armour. It worked, but it didn't make me popular.

I was fine with it 'til I began to notice the few ladies in church who always had a smile and kind words for everybody, who were never ruffled by any situation. They seemed to radiate with this glow of inner peace and self-confidence, a grace and carriage I desperately wanted.

In one of the ladies' meeting, Pastor Lanre's wife, Mummy Felicia, had talked about how the Holy Spirit had changed her completely, even the way she used to talk. So I began quietly emulating her. And even now, when her eldest son seemed to be goading me to let loose my tongue, I held myself in check. How I wish I could scream into his face like I yearned to.

And where would that lead?

I'd only end up feeling bad for hurting Alex and having to apologise *again*. Like one visiting pastor had said, if you don't like apologising, stop doing things that need apologies.

Okay. I know I'm rambling on and on. You must have noticed I do this when I'm nervous and desperately trying to avoid talking about something.

Trust Alex to leave me in knots.

Rowland arrived, and though he was a pleasant company, I knew there wouldn't be any second date. He wasn't even born again. Where do I start from?

Sure, he's a Christian, but there are a billion and one people who go to church every Sunday and throw away God's principles the moment they leave church. I remember when I had this conversation with Simon, back when we had a singles meeting. He had turned to me and asked,

"What kind of husband would you love to have?"

I had said the first thing to pop into my head. "A man who loves and fears God."

"Why?"

I'd mulled over it as I thought. "Two things. When I say love God, I'm talking about when Jesus said if we love Him, we should obey His commandment. Love is not a noun, it's a verb. So a man who claims to love God and has no problem committing adultery or fornication, lying or being a terrible husband and father, is not it."

"And how about when you say fear God?" he had asked, a genuine interest in his eyes.

"I mean a man who fears God and knows Him to be One who disciplines His children. So many Christians use the love of God as a legitimate excuse to do whatever they please, saying God will always love them and forgive. I want a man who does not take God's love for granted and one who fears the consequences of sin."

Simon had paused. "So, a man who knows God as a loving Father *and* a righteous judge that disciplines His children with the rod when they err."

"Exactly. I mean, I can't be too safe. Most Nigerian men have taken it as a norm to continuously cheat on their wives and generally be bad fathers. Me, I can't take it. I know myself very well."

"Are you saying there is no room for mistakes? Your husband must be perfect?"

"No." I had shaken my head furiously. "We can't be perfect, but on this journey, there can be a few mistakes. I can forgive yes, but I don't expect him to see it as a right to do whatever he pleases. That's why he must love God above all else."

Anyways, I know running off my mouth would not be a good idea. Besides, he honestly thought I was with Simon. Why hadn't I cleared up that misunderstanding? It's even sweet he wants to save my soul from sin. Don't laugh at me. I told you I have wacky thoughts, irrational ones at times, and my excuse is the simple fact that I'm a woman. I'm all for feminism, but I love being taken care of too much to put my heart into it. I think women are hundred percent equals with men. We just have different strengths and weaknesses that should complement each other, not lead to full out war. I know. My modern core feminists would be shocked to hear me say this, but I'm being honest here. I know I'm equal to the man, but I have my strengths and weaknesses just like he has his own strengths and weaknesses, and that is that.

I have decided—I'll tell Alex Simon is not my boyfriend or fiancé or whatever he thought.

Will it bring him back to you?

I was inside my car, just preparing to drive home, when I got a text from Mom.

Gone to stay with your Aunt Dorcas. I think it's time for drastic steps.

What?

CHAPTER SEVENTEEN

Aunt Dorcas was already the cause of everything going wrong. If only she hadn't filled Mom's head with bitter thoughts the very first day of the meeting, my parents would have resolved their issues that night. It's already been one month of tension in the house. If she went to stay with her sister, Aunt Dorcas would fill Mom's head with talks of divorce.

Jaja was in his room, playing a game on his phone. He smiled wryly as I stepped into the room, but I could see he was shaken and insecure.

"What happened?" I asked as I dropped my bag.

"I don't know how. Dad came back from work, and he was drunk."

"What?" I screamed.

My dad never gets drunk.

"And when Mom accused him of drinking after work, he started singing this song about woman palaver and how women should stay in the kitchen."

Oh, no!

My mom is staunchly one of those women who, if given the opportunity, would be a strong feminist. She watches too much Oprah. Why can't she be like a normal Nigerian mother with Christian mother arms and no foreign ideologies or ambition? The woman who'd take whatever her husband dishes out because she doesn't know any better and frankly believes she's worth less, so the man can do anything and get away with it?

I turned to go, saw the fear in Jaja's eyes. He is the closest to Mom and the baby of the house. I knew he was missing her already.

I patted his back. "Don't worry. She'll come back."

Dad was in his room, the door locked, and he didn't reply to my knock. Tantrum. I knew it. Normally, when things don't go his way, Dad would sulk and hide in his room. Mom would go to cajole and cheer him up. Men are such babies.

And now, he had locked himself in his room. Was I supposed to baby him now? Who made me mom of the house?

Great! Not only Alex problems, but my parents had to add to the load.

I should just forget Alex and focus on fixing my parents.

Stop longing for what you can't have like a long throat.

Besides, Alex may not believe me if I tell him I'm not dating Simon.

And I really have to do something about Simon. Short of telling him I don't reciprocate the romantic feelings he has for me, what else can I do?

Hmmm! During our double date, he hadn't seemed like someone in love with me despite finding out about me and Alex. Sometimes, I feel Simon is emotionally handicapped. For someone who wrote such a beautiful poem, how can it be so hard for me to see any sign of that love when we're together?

Maybe he's like me, not given to public displays of affection. Yeah, maybe. If so, he has sure built up a huge fort against displaying any feelings for me.

In the five years I've known him, he's never had a girlfriend. Before you start thinking something else, he was in a relationship a while back, but obviously, it ended badly, and he never told me the details.

Somehow, I have to get him interested in somebody else so he'll let go of this ridiculous notion of loving me.

Shouldn't you be happy you have someone?

Seriously. Maybe I should just date him and be with him. He's a good friend, my best friend despite the fact I don't think male and female can be best friends without feelings interrupting. Case in point, Simon.

No.

It would be cruel, settling for him because I can't have the one I really want. Bad recipe.

But I could get him interested in someone else. It would solve his problem, and I'd just be left with my parents and Alex issues to resolve. Who would he possibly like?

I frankly haven't seen him pay any special attention to any girl.

Except you.

Ignore that.

I don't even know his type.

Whatever. There must be someone, and I'll find her. There are thousands of church girls to choose from, and I'd find him the absolute best.

Now that I think about it, I'm actually loving the idea of playing matchmaker. The wheels of my matchmaking brain was rolling rapidly. I love Love.

I'd seen a picture of his ex. Big-boned, heavy in front and behind, the kind of girl who fills out all the places I don't, the kind of girl most Nigerian men love.

Hmmm.

And now, he's in love with me, the slimmest of them all?

Not that I don't love myself, but most of my bras have a little lift on them, if you know what I mean. I'm totally the model type, though I lack the full height, but I got everything else. Growing up had been kind of hard. The teasing from girls with bust and behind, even from boys. Until I learned how to use clothes to my advantage. Anyways, it's water under the bridge, but now, I'm left wondering the kind of girl Simon would like.

Maybe he doesn't have a type.

Okay, I'm going about this the wrong way. Surely, the Holy Spirit will help me. Maybe, with His help, the girl could end up being his wife. It's not like he's not ready for it. He's already thirty-two. Honestly, I don't know what he's waiting for.

You!

Ignore that.

Intercessory prayer alert. One more thing to pray about.

Hmmm.

I hope he makes me his best man. He must. Who else would he possibly pick? I'd just wear a suit and tie and stand beside him.

The sad part is, once he finds her and they get married, I'd cease to be his best friend. No way would I intrude. And I'll have none of the jealous possessiveness female best friends got to have, you know, like when they try to tell the new girl they know all about him and they'll always come first.

What if you're still single by then?

Then I'd be the loneliest girl in Nigeria.

Anyway, I hope to be married by then.

Great plan.

Now, I need a list. Who are the good girls I know who love God, not the ones who come to church just because they want to show off their clothes and find good men?

You know, it can be annoying how they come in, those girls who had several boyfriends and sugar daddies and vacations in the Caribbean, into church and try to steal the few good men who'd decided to heed God's voice from us, the girls who always stayed on track, who didn't wear the most expensive clothes, but somehow, managed without using a man.

O.M.G!

I'm being judgemental. Again.

I'm a Christian. I can't be judgemental. Besides, the one who is yours, is yours. Or so I heard. Until they snatch him.

Back to my list, girls Simon could love and marry.

There's Ibiso, our best soprano singer. She's so nice and has a gentleness I've always admired and try to emulate. She is one of those girls who are so nice, nobody ever has anything bad to say about them. They never say or even think anything bad about anyone. They forgive easily. Me, I had to learn to forgive, and sometimes, it's still a struggle.

Next is Modele. Yes. She's an usher, very dedicated and beautiful. I don't think she has ever missed a service. And I love how she worships, so open and unafraid to cry, kneel, or even lie down anywhere in church.

Wait!

I haven't prayed about this. I'm selecting based on physical. Dammit.

Who besides me would know how church appearances can be deceiving?

Okay.

New plan.

I'd start praying about this tonight and see who the Holy Spirit leads me to.

Shouldn't you also be praying for yourself?

Ha!

No. I have to deal with this Alex thing before I start thinking of marriage. What if a potential husband comes and I don't recognise him because I have a humongous crush on an old school flame?

No.

I'd deal with it first.

Maybe Alex is a potential husband.

Tell that to Chioma, his real girlfriend.

The next day, I barely managed to avoid Alex at the office before heading to church early, gisting with Bianca and other choir members when I saw Jaja's call on my phone.

I picked.

"Mummy has come to pack her things. She's with a big trailer, and ..."

He sniffled, and I knew he was in tears. Damn it. What's wrong with my mom? How could she let one ill-spoken word ruin her marriage?

It's not like she has a bad marriage. My dad never hits her or cheats on her. The picture Aunt Dorcas sent to her is a joke, and she knows it. My dad has been seen countless times with his female students, but we laugh it off because we know he has zero interest in them.

Weird for a man, but it's just how he's wired. Okay, confession, my dad was a virgin when he married my mom, who obviously wasn't, but you know, opposites attract and all that.

What was she thinking?

"Jaja, calm down. I'm coming now." I quickly cut the call and began to head out.

"Glory ..."

Alex.

I turned around and waited hurriedly while he walked towards me.

"I want us to talk," he began.

"Yes, but I don't really have time for that right now—"

He shook his head "I know service is about to start, but—"

"It's not service. I have to head home now before ..."

"Before what?"

I was tempted to tell him. It was just on the tip of my tongue, but my phone rang again, at the same time Simon came out to us.

I held on to him

"Simon, I have to go home now. It's an emergency."

He quickly pulled out his car keys from his pocket. "Let's go."

"Glory, wait, we need to—"

"I don't have time for this right now, Alex," I snapped and got in, ignoring the condemnation in his eyes.

Gosh. Why can't he just read my heart and know it's him I love and want to be with?

Holy Spirit, please tell him I love him.

He stood there, watching us as Simon reversed and drove off. What if he wanted to tell me he loves me?

You wish.

I just can't help feeling I've missed something vital. Oh, well, can't think about this now. Crisis at home.

"What's happening at home?" Simon glanced at me after a while.

And that's when the tears and the whole story poured out of me like spilled milk. I had been holding it inside for so long, it felt good to talk about it.

A big truck was parked outside our gate, and I cringed.

Why did Mom let it get to this? It can't just be because of what Dad said.

I turned to Simon, not wanting him to see the mess about to follow.

"Thank you very much, Simon. I'll call you."

He accepted my dismissal with a nod and drove off.

Jaja was sitting dejected in the parlour, and my heart twisted. Can't she see what she is doing to her son? Jaja is too young for this.

I stormed into her room, and there she was, whirling like a tornado and stuffing things into her box in haste. I knew she'd chosen this time because she didn't want Dad or me around.

"Mom," I called.

She jerked, then smiled as she saw me.

"What are you doing?" I asked quietly.

Her hands faltered as she held a top, then began to shake nervously.

"I can't stay with your father anymore."

"Why?" I leaned on the door.

She glanced nervously behind me, as if expecting somebody to come rescue her.

"You know why. Your father is ..."

"My father? He's your husband first, before he's my father. And don't tell me his careless remark is the only

156

reason for all this. You know very well Dad would never cheat, so don't use that stupid picture as an excuse. Something else is going on, and you need to tell me."

Her nervous smile disappeared. "I just ..."

I lost my patience and snapped. "Don't lie to me, Mom. Your actions right now can't be because of anything Dad has said or done."

She bowed her head, contemplating. Then, she looked at me, her eyes set and serious. I knew I'd lost her.

"You won't understand."

I shook my head and smiled sadly. "No. *You* don't understand. You don't understand the emotional trauma Jaja is going through. Have you become so heartless you don't care about us anymore? What is it?"

She started folding and re-folding the top she held, a guilty look on her face.

"I can't tell you." She shook her head.

Then, I noticed the new, expensive Brazilian weave on her hair. I noticed the fixed lashes and the subtle but composed make-up. My mom was looking hot.

Wait a minute!

"Is this because of a man?" I nearly screamed.

She jumped in fright, grabbed the half-open, half-empty box heedlessly, and made for the door.

I blocked her and held her tightly. "Is this about you? Are you ... cheating on Dad?"

The box dropped from her hands, and tears filled her eyes. "You don't know what you're talking about."

And dread filled my heart.

She hurriedly walked away. I let her go as my mind whirled. It made perfect sense, right?

She couldn't possibly be making all of this ruckus just because of one careless statement or a picture.

But how ... how did this happen?

My parents are happily married, or so I thought.

Was it all a sham? Or had my dad's absent-mindedness driven her to another man's arms?

Let me tell you, diary, it's hard to imagine your mom with another man. Normally, the man is the serial cheater so we don't get surprised if he suddenly says he's taking a second wife or his mistress is pregnant. Heck, most Nigerian women prepare for this eventuality.

But it's a different case when your mom is the one doing the cheating.

Okay, I have not verified it, but her reaction made it seem true. Why else would she be so eager to leave her husband if not for another man?

Still, it is so hard to believe. Women are mostly loyal, especially Nigerian women. The scandal alone would never let them have affairs, never mind how it's commonplace for men to leave their families for other women.

I heard her whispers to Jaja, and then the drone of the truck as it drove off.

My poor dad.

Glory, don't judge based on assumptions.

Okay. I'm not certain of anything, even though she is obstinate about leaving her husband and looking hot. Clearly, I would have to take investigative steps to solve this. My parents' marriage had always been a good model, and I wouldn't let it crash without a fight. Whatever was her reason, I would find it out and destroy it.

I prepared yam and egg sauce and left Jaja busy with DSTV as I retreated to my room.

Then, I saw the missed calls from Alex. And a text, *'Call me. I'm worried.'*

What would I tell him if I called?

My dad's horn blared by seven p.m., and I waited patiently 'til he'd had dinner before I approached him in his room.

"Mom came with a truck to pack her things today."

He didn't move, just stood so still that, for a moment, I was afraid he hadn't heard. Then, he turned to me, and I saw the look of hopelessness and confusion in his eyes. He really loved my mom.

"How ..." He cleared his throat. "How can I ... stop her?"

I had no answer. But I knew there was no way I'd let her ruin this home.

CHAPTER EIGHTEEN

Alex was waiting at the car park as I drove into the office parking lot. I smiled shyly as I alighted, blithely aware I hadn't returned his calls or replied his text.

"Good morning," I called out.

"Good morning. I was worried. Is everything all right?" he asked as he searched my face.

My sweet love.

Great, now I was saying those crappy, cliché romantic drivels.

"It's all good. It was just a family emergency."

He picked up my pace and followed me into the building.

"Anything I can do to help?"

Yes. Love me. Stand by me.

"Just pray about it."

He nodded and stepped aside to open the departmental door for me. Then held my hands as I tried to walk past.

"I just ... I want to apologise. I accused you of double dating, and that wasn't fair."

He looked at me earnestly, and my heart lurched.

Now! I should tell him I'm not dating Simon.

I opened my mouth, just as Georgewill stormed in, whistling a gay tune.

The moment was lost.

He dropped my hands. "I'll see you later."

It wouldn't do for Georgewill, the office's biggest gossip, to see us together with even a hint of intimate interaction. The rumour would spread by morning, and Alex didn't need that. Already, I'd succeeded in keeping the fact we attended the same church from them. If they found out, the speculations would be flying everywhere.

I sighed as I watched him walk away, then entered my office and sat down, flexing my finger as I said a short prayer.

"Hmmmm."

Georgewill.

"What?" I glared at him.

"Nothing, oh."

I looked at him, refusing to blink and back down. He held his hands up in mock surrender.

"You too like talk," I cautioned and switched on my system.

"I haven't said anything. Besides, there's something else, better gist."

"Uh, huh." I shook my head, disinterested. More office gossip that I always avoided.

"You're not even paying attention."

"Uh, huh. Because I'm not interested." To prove my point, I plugged in my earpiece and listened to my praise playlist.

I'd learned never to involve myself in office gossip. Not only did it sour relationships, it was always mostly false speculations. Like the one time Juliet had spread the rumour the Head of Operations, a married woman of thirty years with no child, was pregnant for her driver.

Until we saw the baby who looked exactly like her husband and felt silly. That was even the good one. Conclusion was, gossip caused more harm than good and made the gossipers feel supercilious, like they were morally more upright than the persons they talked about. I so wasn't interested.

It was mid-afternoon, just when I was leaving for lunch, when I got a text from Alex.

'I'd like us to talk. 7pm. Blue Elephant.'

OMG! Blue elephant? That was a very popular five-star restaurant. Wait!

Was this a date?

Why was he so keen to talk to me all of a sudden?

Maybe he wanted to tell me he still had feelings for me. How sweet would it be?

What else could it possibly be? He wasn't even upset I'd been kind of mean and inattentive lately.

But what about Chioma?

Maybe I had been living in assumptions all this while, just like he had been thinking I'm dating Simon. Maybe he'd found out the truth, and ...

OMG!

He totally wanted to tell me he still likes me. Maybe even loves me.

The glee was hard to contain ... Until I looked at my nails. I hadn't done my nails in ages. They were chipped and dull.

Why didn't he tell me on time?

I wouldn't have worn this old shirt and trouser, or, kill me now, my comfortable stump heel that always makes me feel like an olden days school teacher. It always makes this thumping noise I hate.

Oh, God!

And my perfume is not in my bag. I have no make-up with me. The day I change my bag and forget to transfer essentials like my powder, foundation, and lipstick.

Even my make-up is crudely applied because of the rush preparing Jaja's breakfast.

Why?

Today of all days.

Maybe I can quickly rush home and change?

No.

If I do get home, I'd be tempted to take a bath and do a total make-over and end up late, and who knows what Alex will think? I don't want him to think I'm standing him up.

Or I could re-schedule.

What if he thinks I'm just trying to blow him off?

No. I have to find a way to make this outfit work.

And Juliet walked in. I smiled and heaved a sigh of relief. Her bag was always literally full of make-up, and her skin tone was close to mine, so I could use some of hers.

And didn't I still have last Sunday's heels in the back seat of my car?

This could totally work.

Oh my gosh!

At last!

Of course, the day dragged slowly, and I almost expired as the clock ticked slowly and slowly and on and on.

Finally, it was five-thirty, and all it took to lure Juliet to the bathroom to do my make-up expertly was "I have a hot date."

By the time I stepped out an hour later, I looked and felt so much more beautiful and confident. I walked slowly and regally, feeling like a model, a queen. I even felt like cupping my hands and doing the models' wave.

I badgered Julie to take pictures, and I took about a hundred selfies to remember this moment. It's not every day your dream comes true.

I hope he also keeps me well-informed when he proposes so I can look fab and have a professional photographer take pictures. Oh, how I hate those blurry phone pictures of engagements, with the oblivious girls looking like just any other day with bad nails.

Georgewill snorts as we pose and snap. Men! They can never understand.

My phone vibed, and another text from Alex came in. '*Already there. Waiting for you.*'

My heart panged as I looked at the picture of my parents on my wallpaper. I needed to fix them so we could all be happy as I was.

I quickly texted back, '*On my way.*'

"Details tomorrow?" Juliet asked.

I smiled and say nothing. I could give her details, but I wasn't certain I'd like the office to know Alex and I were now an item until we were ready to take it to the next level.

By the time I got to the restaurant, my hands were shaking, and my heart was racing wildly. It was just too beautiful. After all these years, we'd found each other.

God, I'm so happy. Tears filled my eyes, and I carefully dabbed at them with my handkerchief. Didn't need tears smudging my mascara or my eye shadow.

Blue Elephant is an upscale, highly expensive hub. I'd only been there once, during an Award Gala, and the place is moderately seated, the lights are low, yellow and blue, casting a romantic feel to the atmosphere.

There he was—the love of my life, sitting beside the window and looking around. He looked so handsome in his pale blue suit. I will insist he wears this colour on our wedding day.

You know how they say a woman dreams of her wedding right from when she's little? They're totally right.

I had even planned and decorated my house in my head, and watching Alex sit there, I mentally change the colour of our bedroom walls to pale blue and the lights to pale yellow and red. I wanted to preserve this moment.

He looked up and spotted me, then smiled and stood, a bit shyly.

Awwww!

He was nervous, too.

Oh, baby, I love you, too.

This was going to make an epic story for our grand-kids. I'd tell them how their granddad was so nervous the day he told me he loved me.

He held my hands lightly and smiled his special smile that always lights me up.

"I hope I didn't keep you waiting too long." My voice was soft and breathy, like a princess.

"It's fine. I would ask how was work, but ..."

We laughed together.

"But seriously, how was work?" He signalled to a waiter as we sat.

"It was good. Kind of normal."

"You look amazing, by the way. It's one thing I love. You always look amazing."

I smiled and preened. He'll never know the stress I went through to achieve this effortless look. I flipped my hair casually so my good side and my dangling earrings showed.

The waiter came, and we placed an order.

Alex looked seriously at me as he left. "I have to apologise formally for the way I treated you in secondary school ..."

He struggled to continue. Frankly, I'd been a bit scared about that side of him. Not that he'd shown me any reason to worry since he'd come back, but ...

"I have no explanations. I think I was just obsessed with you, and it was an unhealthy way to love someone."

Obsessed? Why?

He smiled and answered my unspoken question.

"I grew up distant from my parents. Their work in the ministry and church kept them so busy and always travelling, I rarely saw them. My aunts practically raised me. I guess it's why I was so possessive, I just didn't ... I wanted to have somebody to myself, somebody who would put me in the centre of their world and shun every other thing."

I held his hands on the table. "I understand."

He nodded, then smiled, obviously relieved to get that part out of the way.

Our meals arrived, and I dug in eagerly. I'd been so tied up about the date, I'd forgotten to eat, and they had this heavenly pasta that practically melted like butter in my mouth, and I closed my eyes to savour the taste.

And opened them to find Alex staring at my lips, a look of hunger in his eyes. I looked away quickly and began to take dainty bites.

"The food here is so great," he said.

"And ridiculously expensive."

"It is a five-star restaurant."

Okay, forgive me. I know I'm with the love of my life and therefore, under a lot of pressure, but I can't just ignore the heavenly dishes the waiter keeps placing in front of me, each one so delicious and small, I'm able to eat it all without being too full. Talk about quality service.

I could eat like this the rest of my life. And as soon as the last course was cleared, I knew we were about to get serious.

Surreptitiously, I checked my profile in the reflection from the window to make sure everything was in place.

Then, he leaned towards me and said ...

"What do you think of Chioma?"

My smile faltered. Why was he asking about Chioma?

I took a sip of my Chapman, stalling for time. What did I think of her? Man-stealer was the first word coming to my head.

So I said, "She's a great person. I've known her for years."

"Yes, but what do you really think of her?"

He was looking at me intently, expectantly.

Oh, baby, why can't we talk about me? What does she have that I don't?

"Um ... any particular reason for this interest in her?"

I mean, I'm seated here, beautiful, with a heart full of love directed at you, and you're more interested in another girl?

As you can guess, the night went downhill from there. I must be a good actress; otherwise, I don't know how I was able to keep the tears from falling down my face.

All of this ... to freaking ask my opinion on his dating Chioma?

How oblivious and cruel could he be?

Like, hello? I'm here, pining for you, and you're asking my opinion on Chioma?

Damn.

I acted all irritated and hastily told him I needed to rest. I saw the disappointment in his eyes, and it made me even angrier. What did he expect? That I'd just be a good friend to him?

What?

Should I be every boy's best friend? No. Let Chioma be his friend and girlfriend. I didn't give a damn.

Somehow, when I did get home, I couldn't cry. The tears had all dried up, and I was numb inside. I couldn't feel a thing. I wasn't not angry, or depressed, or insanely jealous. Nothing, Zilch.

CHAPTER NINETEEN

So today, I find myself with my dad in his car outside Aunt Dorcas' house, spying on my Mom. How did I get here? Let's start from the beginning.

I woke up feeling empty and frustrated, which was new because I never, ever, feel frustrated. As a Christian, I'd learned long ago that no situation was worth that feeling; God always makes a way. It's just, the events of the past night had practically drained me of the tiny hope I had been harbouring.

Just as I was heading out, I found my dad sitting in the parlour in his pyjamas and watching, you won't believe it, Disney, of all things. What the hey?

He never watched animation. Ever. And why was he not dressed up for work?

Knowing fully that he'd suck me into his la la land, I dared to ask, "What's wrong, Dad?"

And he, of course, told me the shocker. Okay, to avoid his sniffles and suspicious red eyes, let me give you my own version.

Apparently, while Alex had been twisting the knife in my heart last night, my dad had gone to talk to my mom in Aunt Dorcas' house, and she had blatantly refused to see him even though he'd waited for three hours.

His eyes were red, and I knew my dad, the softie, was near tears.

So therefore, I was near tears, hence the frustration. Suddenly, I felt tired and overwhelmed with all the things going wrong—first my parents, then Simon and Alex. God, I needed a break.

Seeing my dad miss work because of heartbreak made me do another unthinkable. "So what do you want to do?"

And he looked at me with his brown eyes. "It must be because of a man. It's the only logical conclusion."

Uh, oh!

Now, he's also suspecting my mom.

I laughed nervously and squeaked "No. Mom would never do that."

He bent his head. "It's the only explanation that makes sense. She ... She has always complained I don't see her enough. She always says I leave my head in the clouds too much. I've neglected her, and she's found somebody better, who will love her like she deserves."

And then, he really broke down, and I was patting his back, thinking how absurd it would seem to outsiders that my dad cried, in front of me. His sobs were so gut-wrenching.

"Mom would never betray you like this. I know it."

He cleaned his eyes and held himself up. "I never deserved her. Now, she's gone."

That's when I snapped. "Stop being a cry-baby and find a way to get your woman back. Do you want another man to take what's yours?"

He stared into the screen for a long while and finally muttered, "Whoever he is, I'll kill him."

I laughed. It was so like the whole 'I don't know who you are, but I'll find you and I'll kill you' movie thing.

Better not get him so excited.

"Dad, I meant you should try to win her back. Besides, you're not sure, and you've not seen her with any guy. So who you going to kill, huh?"

And then, he said it. "I'll find out. I'll follow her, and find out who he is."

"You mean you'll spy on Mom?"

He didn't reply, his mind obviously plotting.

Great!

Why did I open my big mouth?

"Dad ..." I shook his shoulders until he focused on me.

"Don't do anything stu—" Was I about to say stupid? He was still my dad. "Don't do anything unwise. In fact, let me know of your plans. I'll help you."

Translation: 'I'll keep an eye on you and stop you from doing something foolish.'

"You will?"

He looked so hopeful, and I nodded.

Now I'll have to babysit my dad, too. Hello, people. Why leave all these responsibilities to me? Sometimes, I want to be a baby, too.

Anyways, heading to the office, the ice in my heart started to shake in trepidation; it was like the theme song in Game of Thrones was playing loudly in my head.

It's so hard. Why did I have to work with him? What a twist of cruel fate.

The worst part was I had to pretend all was cool between us.

And, yeah, Juliet pounced on me the minute I opened my eyes after a short prayer.

"How was it?"

I shook my head. "Not as I thought."

"What? What happened?"

"It wasn't what I thought it was. That's all I can say."

Her smile dimmed. "I'm so sorry."

"It's cool. No biggie."

And the awkwardness began. Alex strolled by to my manager's office, and my heart thudded so heavily, it was painful, and tears filled my eyes as I looked at my screen.

Then, I got a text from Alex. 'Hi.'

I was so angry, and I hissed so long, Georgewill looked at me, surprised.

"Sister Glo, is that hiss from you?"

I ignored him. Juliet shot him a dark look.

"What?" he cried.

Men are so oblivious. Idiots, all of them.

Careful there. You're getting bitter.

And the tears rolled out again, and I headed to the bathroom. I know, I know. I guess my feelings for Alex were really deep, and somehow, I must have held out hope his relationship with Chioma was just in my head. But hearing him confirm it just plain killed me.

What do I do now?

Focus on your God, your family, and career. Time will heal these wounds.

Seeing them every day in church and work would make the healing really slow, but what choice did I have short of resigning and changing church?

That, I would never do. I wouldn't let them run me out of my job and my church family. Never.

And when they get serious?

I'd just suck it up and deal with it. I gave it three weeks, and I'd be so over it.

You mean three months or years?

Whatever. I'd be over it, and that was that.

Now, to avoid speaking to him or running into him ... my office was an open-planned space, and though Alex's was closed and all, he could raise his head and see me walk through the Operations Exit before I could get to the staircase.

I didn't even want him to see me leave. He may come to talk to me in the spirit of supposed friendship. Or he may just open his door and run into me at the staircase or car park.

As I sat stewing, I notice the Head of Operations heading into his office, and I gleefully shot up and made my escape.

I called my dad as soon as I got into my car to check up on him.

"Yes, I won't be home early today. Please go and stay with Jaja," he says impatiently.

"Jaja is a big boy. He doesn't need a babysitter. Where are you going?"

A pause. And this pause made me suspicious.

"Dad, where are you?"

"None of your business. Stop questioning me. I am your father."

I heard the honk of a truck. And I knew. I just knew.

"Are you at Aunt Dorcas' place?"

He laughed nervously. "No. I left there hours ago."

"Wait. Hours ago?"

"I went to see your mother. She kept me waiting for five hours and never came down."

"So where are you now?"

"None of your business." He cut the call.

I muttered as I drove, angry. Why couldn't my parents just be normal? Why? I'd give anything for them to the wrapper-tying, always shouting kind of parents.

All of that doesn't matter because I drove to Aunt Dorcas', and sure enough, there's my dad's car, parked just a little distance from her gate.

I parked behind him, walked up to his car, and peered in. He was just sitting there, drinking from a foam cup and staring at Aunt Dorcas' gate with all concentration.

I knocked loudly, and he yelped, spilling some of his drink on his hands and trousers. His eyes bulged as he saw me, and he undid the locks, so I entered and slammed the door.

"Be careful."

I rolled my eyes, prepared to give my father the yell of a lifetime. "What are you doing here? Just when did you become a stalker? How is this going to help?"

"One question at a time." He dropped the cup in the holder and looked sheepishly at me. I see Jaja's resemblance to him, and my anger dissipates. "See, I know she'll soon go out. So I'll follow her so I can find out who that man is."

I shook my head sadly. "It's an assumption, Dad. You're assuming she's seeing someone else. And how do you know she'll soon leave the house?"

"I waited for five hours in her parlour, playing Candy Crush. Then, I heard her tell the security to expect Kunle. Who is Kunle, if not the man she's seeing?"

I bent my head, put my hand on my chin, and pretended to think about it. "So you follow her and this Kunle guy, then interrupt their date and beat Kunle up, assuming he's weaker. Then what? Will it make Mom fall into your arms?"

"Well, what else do I do? I can't just sit at home twiddling my thumbs. Please go home. I promise I won't fight with any man I may see her with. Go."

He had that look of authority, and I was just his daughter, so I opened the door and slid out. "Just be careful."

"Yes. And remember I'm still your father."

I roll my eyes. Yes, my father, and behaving like a lovelorn boy.

CHAPTER TWENTY

It had been three days, and I still couldn't feel a thing. I was still completely numb, smiling when the situation called for it and nothing else. Even seeing Alex did nothing. That's how I was able to get though seeing him in the office.

I'd ignored his texts and calls so much, he had stopped.

Even Georgewill and Juliet knew something was wrong. I'd been avoiding Simon like the plague.

Why was my life suddenly like this?

Mom was still doing whatever she was doing without Dad in her life. My father kept shrinking before my eyes, and I was torn.

At home, I tried to keep my father out of trouble, and avoid Alex at work and in church.

Not that it was so easy avoiding him. Alex, I mean. How did you avoid someone who still thought you were a good friend?

Not easy. I hadn't replied to any of his texts, kept my butt on my seat at work. Luckily, there'd been no need for work to make us talk or such. Seriously, it was exhausting, and I was almost caving. I was thinking when my luck ran out and he eventually cornered me, I'd just lie and say my phone is bad or something. I couldn't reply texts and receive or make calls.

Damn.

Okay. It's just a small white lie. God will understand.

Yes. That is how it starts ... until I become a big fat liar.

What the hey? Why should I lie?

I'd just tell him the truth. Wait, no. It would be embarrassing. I'd tell him a version of the truth. It was still lying.

Oh, this is too hard to think about.

And my dad, he registered for the gym yesterday. Yes. My dear, fifty-eight years old, pot-bellied dad. He refused to talk about his stalking experience the other day. So I suspected Kunle, Mom's supposed boyfriend, must have been a young man, and he planned to get fit to either impress my mom or take Kunle down.

Oh, you needed to see him in his gym sweats. He even tied a sweat band on his forehead and wore elbow and ankle sweat bands. It was so comical and endearing. Never mind how my mom had been harping on him to eat well and exercise for years before now.

Maybe his hopes to become buff so Mom will see him as handsome again and take him back would work.

It's not like we were not having the same suspicions. It's just that I'm handling mine better while Dad is going all Commando. The rational thing would be to force his way in to see Mom and have a talk. It's cruel of her to just keep him hanging like this.

At least, she's started talking to Jaja on the phone about the whole issue, and he's feeling better about the whole thing. She'd even invited him to spend the weekend with her, and there he'd gone at the moment, which I was grateful for.

Lately, he's decided to become a chef and has been rummaging in the kitchen. The other day, he made runny eggs and used so much pepper, the house was filled with this stench that made us cough for hours. Then, he cooked rice and put every spice in the cupboard in it. Suffice it to say it was inedible and promptly thrown out. Now he's gone, the kitchen and walls in the house can breathe fine.

Me, I've decided to find a way to talk to Mom about Dad. If she's serious about leaving him, she should let him know so he can start healing and getting closure.

What if she's serious? What if it wasn't one of these attention-seeking stunts women pull? Or a mid-life crisis?

Great!

My dad would be too heartbroken. It can't be real. Short of kidnapping her, I'd do everything to make sure their marriage didn't end.

I refuse to lose all the important relationships in my life. My parents, Alex, even Simon. I hadn't really talked with Simon ever since the day he'd dropped me off. I didn't know how to handle him. I'd started praying about finding a wife for him. I know he's ready. He has a good job, good enough to take care of a family. He has healthy savings, so I know he's got money for a wedding.

Definitely time.

He's your best friend. Why not marry him?

Because I'm not in love with him. It's not every boy-girl relationship that must end with romance or sex, you know. Simon has been like an older brother to me. I thought we were on the same page until I saw his love note.

Oh, why did he fall in love with me?

I'd start talking to him about a wife as subtly as I could. Or I'd just come out and say it. I needed to stop walking on eggshells around him. He was my brother, my best friend. Besides, it's the way I would normally do it if I hadn't seen his note.

So, it would have to do. Wish me luck.

I got to church and met Simon laughing with a group of the instrumentalists.

Sure enough, I joined them and smiled cordially, tapped my foot all through rehearsals, impatient.

As he drove me home, I was still nervously tapping my foot until he turned to me.

"Okay. Out with it. What do you have to say?"

I stuttered at first. "Nothing. Just ..."

"Glory, I know when you have something on your mind and you can't wait to share. Just tell me ..."

"But ..."

"Remember when I ate garlic and had garlic breath for a whole day, and you wanted to tell me?"

I smiled as I recollected the halting, awkward, bumpy experience. As a friend, certain topics have always made me feel uncomfortable.

I took a deep breath and jumped right in. "I think you should get married."

He stopped for a moment, then laughed and laughed.

"What ... Why the sudden need for me to change my marital condition?"

"I don't know ..."

I picked at unseen lint in my ash skirt, hoping he didn't begin to think I was talking about him getting married to me, like I was propositioning him. Or even see it as an affirmation that I returned his feelings. "I mean, there are a lot, a lot of good girls you know, and you're already thirty ..."

"Wait. Are you serious?"

"Yes."

He looked away thoughtfully as I twisted and untwisted the hem of my skirt.

Finally, he said the shocking words. "I'm way ahead of you. I'm getting married this year."

"What?" My eyes were round as saucers. "To who?" I asked as my heart threaded a dull, steady beat.

"A friend. She just doesn't know it yet."

Oh my *gosh*.

He was talking about me. And he was so certain I would say yes.

What do I do, what do I do?

"What friend is it? And how are you so certain she'll say yes to you?"

He smiled with so much confidence, it was annoying. "She loves me. She just doesn't know it yet."

Hmmm!

Where had this pig-headedness come from?

He actually thought I'm secretly or unknowingly in love with him?

But he knew about my crush on Alex.

Crush? Don't you mean love?

Ignore the voice in my head.

How can he think I love him when he knows about Alex?

Sure enough, the next person he asked about is the devil, not that Alex was a devil.

"And how is our high school boyfriend? You know, you've been awfully quiet about him. What's up with that?

"Nothing is up. He's fine."

"Uh, huh. And what happened to the feelings creeping back up, the left-over feelings induced by nostalgia?

Was this his way of probing if I still liked Alex before asking me to marry him?

Wait!

I knew how this could work to my advantage. I'd just pretend to still have intense feelings for Alex, and maybe he'd back off.

Pretend to still love Alex? Pretend?

Moving on.

But what if he didn't already know about Alex's intentions towards Chioma? They hadn't come out publicly about their relationship, so maybe he didn't have a clue yet.

"Actually, I had a date with him last week."

He laughed spuriously, obviously excited.

See, this is the thing I don't understand. If he loved me, why wasn't he upset about it? He shouldn't be so happy. Maybe he thought my feelings for Alex were shallow and the hidden love I had for him was the real deal.

"Good for you. Very soon, you two will be loving all up again."

Despite the absurdity of it all, I laughed. I had missed this, this easy camaraderie between us. At the moment, I felt this burst of love, agape love, and without thinking, I said it.

"I've missed you, Simon. Why haven't we hung out in a while?"

He smiled.

"Work. Family. And don't forget, your drama at home. Is your mom back?"

I snorted. "She's now in my aunt's house. Jaja went to spend the weekend with them. Which is good for me because he's attempting to be a chef, with an obsessive predilection for pepper."

We laughed.

"But your mom has not said anything regarding why she left?"

I shook my head, and he looked at me, serious.

"Have you talked to her?"

No.

"I haven't had time," I replied.

He parked beside my gate and turned to me. "You're upset. You're mad at her for leaving without explanation."

"No. I'm just confused."

"So why haven't you talked to her about it?"

"Nothing. I just haven't seen her since ..."

He snorted. "Go and see her. Talk about it."

I nodded while alighting. Then stopped. "Do I know this girl you're talking about?"

He smiled mischievously. "Yes."

And I went into my house to meet another shocker.

Just as I showered and was getting ready for bed, Dad came in with a package which he dropped on the bed.

"I got you something."

I opened the package to see this new set of extremely colourful gym clothes, elastic head bands and elbow bands, with sneakers.

I looked at him with surprise.

"I paid for gym membership for you," he said with a huge smile, looking at me expectantly.

"Dad, I don't have time to gym, except on weekends. Besides, I'm not a fan of exercise. I don't have—"

"Okay. I've thought about this. How about three evenings, maybe weekends?"

"I'll think about it."

He ambled out, humming excitedly. No way was I going to a gym to sweat it out with my dad who, by the way, was only getting buffed up so he could beat up his wife's imaginary or real lover.

Simon was right. I should see my mom, talk to her.

Why would she just up and leave her home like that?

On Sunday, service was great, one of those occasions when Pastor Lanre's wife preached and got the church all riled up and inspired.

I felt good, started humming on the inside. Not even the sight of Alex and Chioma talking after church could disturb me.

"Glory ..." Chioma called out.

I strolled towards them, trying to walk confidently despite the pinch of my six-inch heels. Why do we go through this stress?

Oh, yes. They make us walk beautifully.

By the time I got there, Alex just looked into his phone.

"Hi ..." I said with a smile.

He nodded and continued to peer into his phone.

Chioma was gaily smiling up at me. "What's up?"

"I'm good." I leaned beside the pillar.

"When is this meeting going to end? I'm so hungry, and we're going to Genesis after now."

I ignored the stab in my heart. Too much information, Chioma. Now, I'd have images of them, the beautiful ones, having lunch.

Damn it!

"It's just the single ladies meeting. You know Mrs. Okoro is not the type to prolong meetings," I managed to reply.

"Yeah."

She whispered something into Alex's ear, and he grinned, still looking into his phone.

Did they bring me here just to torture me? Yes. I get it. You're a happy beautiful couple. No need to rub it in my face.

I hissed and walked away without another word. And my phone buzzed in my hands, a text from Alex.

'You're avoiding me. What did I do?'

I typed furiously back.

'We work together and attend the same church. Maybe you're not trying hard enough. Have fun at Genesis.'

I hit send.

Then, I cringed. Why had I put the part about Genesis? Now he'd think I'm jealous or something.

Whatever.

I didn't care what he thought.

I headed off to the single ladies meeting, and we talked about having a rally to publicise the upcoming program for singles.

As they talked, my eyes wandered over to the other group of women at the third row. The married women. Most had that glow, some were pregnant, and I felt envious. Frankly, I was tired of being in the Single Ladies Department. I wanted to be in the Married Women Department. Was it too much?

Then stop falling in love with people you can't have.

Why was I so dramatic? Why couldn't I just fall in love with Simon and tie up my life with a pretty red bow? It would solve all my problems.

But no. I had to try to attain for what I didn't have. Why did I do this to myself? Why couldn't I just be a normal girl? Simon was perfect for me—he's born again, kind, financially able to take care of a family, handsome, courteous, and thoughtful.

Even as I listed them, I knew deep inside of me he was a brother.

God!

Moral codes could be such a bother sometimes. Otherwise, I'd be marrying him and not caring if it's right or not.

Whatever!

I had to find another way to dissuade his attentions. Maybe if I threw another girl at him, a good girl, one he would normally overlook but who would actually be perfect for him.

And this was my perfect opportunity, the perfect place to look. As Mrs. Okoro talked, I surreptitiously craned my neck, searching for the perfect girl for Simon.

Hmmmm!

Not to brag, but my church girls are beautiful, every single one of them. And their dress style is wow.

In the midst of all these girls was a perfect wife for Simon. I just had to find her.

Holy Spirit, help me.

And suddenly, the girl beside me asked for a pen, and it's like a blinding flash.

Modele.

The usher I had considered previously.

As she scribbled furiously into her note, I glanced at her profile. She's beautiful, reserved, but she has mischievous eyes. She would make a great potential wife.

Muttering a quick prayer, I waited 'til the closing prayer had been said, then turned to her as she stood to leave, returning my pen.

"Hey, are you busy on Thursday afternoon?"

I know she's an entrepreneur who works from home, so she can't have any excuse.

She smiled shyly.

"No. I'm kind of taking a break this week. Had a big order last month that kept me tied to my machine throughout."

"Great. This means you can join me for dinner."

No need to mention Simon would be there.

She frowned slightly, probably wondering why I was inviting her for dinner.

Okay, I know I've never really talked much to her, or, now that I think about it, other girls in church except those in choir.

Well, it's hardly my fault. My church is so big, and the choir itself is also vast.

Besides, I think secondary school has made me a one-friend person. I don't feel the need to surround myself with thousands of girlfriends.

In fact, I hardly have any good friends except Simon.

We talk and smile in church, but mostly, that's it. I have no girls coming over, none to go over to.

Wow!

Simon is my only friend.

How did I not notice it?

Maybe I lost interest and the ease of making friends all those lonely years in secondary school.

I will make more friends—female friends, to be exact.

I smiled at Modele, resolved, and collected her number to let her know the venue.

Even if it didn't work out between her and Simon, I'd still keep her as a friend.

Bianca rushed up to me just as I got to the exit door.

"Glory, wait ..."

I waited patiently as she walked delicately in her eight-inch heels. Bianca was that type of girl, the one who wore impossibly high heels all day without feeling any twinge.

She inspired me to start wearing heels, and I remember how I struggled initially. She smiled as she caught up to me.

Chioma and Bianca are the two girls I connect with most in the choir, despite the fact they're both Soprano singers and I'm Alto.

"Why did you invite Modele and not me for dinner?"

How ...

"She's my friend, too, you know. So she asked me if I was going to be there. Shebi, I've been telling you to take me out since, and you asked Modele and not me? When did she become a better friend than me? In fact, when did she become a friend at all?"

Typical Bianca. She's one of those confrontational types, speaks her mind always, always forthright kind of girls. Honestly, I see her as the troublesome type; her frankness can be misconstrued as rude.

And she used to be a fighter. She always regales us with talks of fights she used to be involved in right from childhood, even with guys. Growing up in the shanty toughened her up.

"It's not really a ... you know what, you can come. I'll just make it a get together in my house. We've been complaining of how we hardly spend time together. But now, I need someone to do the cooking."

"Ah. I'm here. You've forgotten me?"

I smiled and tapped her arm. She was a caterer.

"Oya, let's start inviting. I hope you won't charge me too much." I smiled at her.

She opened her bag, brought out her notepad, and started taking notes. "It depends. How many people?"

"I don't know for certain. Just invite our friends in Choir and Ushering Department."

"Only girls?"

No. Then Simon wouldn't be there. "No. Guys included."

"Okay."

She zoomed off into the crowd, inviting and smiling as she went. She met the row of choristers and instrumentalists, raised her hand, and as soon as everyone was quiet, I saw her speak quite animatedly. They all cheered, then she turned, winked at me, and gave me a thumbs up.

What the hey? Did she just invite the entire choir unit?

Bianca left the choristers and started moving towards the Ushering department's meeting that just rounded up.

Oh, no. She talked to all of them, and they cheered.

What? Did she just invite the entire Choir Unit *and* Ushering Department?

What had I done, unleashing Bianca as my party planner? She's so friendly, I knew she'd invite the entire church.

Now I had a huge party to host and basically no preparations. How did a dinner for three in a fast food evolve into a dinner for a crowd in my house?

I let Bianca put words in my mouth. But anyway, as long as it helped me fix Simon up with Modele and make him forget about me romantically, it would be worth it.

Bianca rushed up to me. "Faith says she can bring finger foods ..."

Faith beside her beamed. "What kind do you like? Meat pie, samosa, spring rolls ..."

I looked at Bianca in awe. How was she able to just have a flowing easy relationship with everybody? "Just bring anything."

Bianca presented another girl, a familiar face in church. "Briggs is a pepper soup specialist and a DJ."

"I don't need a DJ. I have a good sound system in my house."

Briggs smiled. "Then I'll just be in charge of music. It's on Friday, right?"

"It's actually Thurs—" I start.

"Of course it's Friday," Bianca cuts in. "Who would throw a party on Thursday? Besides, we need to think about themes and colour scheme for the party. I'm thinking red..."

She continued as they walked away, taking charge of my party. This was good, anyways, as I didn't have all the time to personally take care of details.

Simon walked up to me. "I heard you're throwing a big party with a white and red theme."

"Oh my gosh, Bianca will kill me. There's no colour scheme or party theme. That's all Bianca. She has taken over everything."

He snorted. "Of course she took over your party. She's like a regular Dracula. It's her personality. Why the sudden need for a get together?"

To fix you up with Modele.

"Oh ... nothing really. Just an impromptu urge. You're coming, right?"

"And miss your hosting skills combined with Bianca's food? Wouldn't miss it."

Good. Plan in motion. Dad wouldn't object to my get-together. In fact, he'd been bemoaning my lack of close female friends. Simon, apparently, was not enough for him.

According to him, my mom was leader of a huge clique when she was my age.

Well, not my fault I'm socially awkward and not at ease with making new friends.

"So, have you gone to see your mom yet?" Simon asked.

"No."

He nodded absently.

"What?" I yelled.

"Nothing. I didn't say anything."

I narrowed my eyes at him. "No, but you were thinking it. I am *not* angry with my mom."

"I believe you. Even though I know you're lying to yourself."

"Whatever."

He laughed and calmly dropped me off.

And of course, I couldn't relax even though the evening was a cool one.

I had to see my mom, just to prove Simon wrong. I wasn't secretly mad at her.

Why would I be? It wasn't burdensome taking care of my dad and Jaja. It wasn't enough reason to be mad at her.

What if you feel betrayed that she abandoned her family for no apparent reason?

Only one way to find out.

I could go see her under the pretext of picking Jaja up.

It's how I found myself in Aunt Dorcas'.

Obviously, Mom has put only my father's name in the Blacklist because the security promptly lets me in without any fuss.

Mom and Jaja were eating from a big bowl of popcorn and watching a movie. She smiled as she saw me and came to hug me.

I waited for the incredible anger Simon talked about, but there was just a slight tightening of my chest.

"Thank God you're here. I was just about to—" she began.

And the words burst out of me. "When are you coming back home?"

Her smile faded, and she dropped her arms. "I'm not sure about that."

"You're not sure? Do me a favour, Mom. How about you talk to your husband? He's your husband, not mine. Stop leaving your responsibility for me. Dad has never done anything evil to you, so why are you punishing him like this?"

"You can't speak to me like this. I'm still your mother."

"Then act like one." I was breathing hard and staring at her, and then, I realised—there's the anger Simon was talking about. And I knew instantly I felt abandoned, rejected, and I'd been hiding it under a false sense of normalcy.

"Jaja, go get your things," she said as he rose.

"Welcome, sister ..." he mumbled as he walked out, obviously embarrassed to be present during our fight.

"You can't disrespect me like that. I know—" my mom starts.

I cut in. "I know, and I'm sorry, Mom. I know I shouldn't interfere in your marriage, but I just feel abandoned."

"Oh, sweetie ... it's not like that. I just, I can't tell you about it. Not yet." She held my arms earnestly.

Okay, I know we seem pretty close, but my mom had me at a very young age, and she raised me like a friend, or a younger sister instead of a daughter.

"Just do me this favour and talk to Dad, please. He's been here several times, and you've refused to see him."

She looked away. "I'll try."

Jaja came back in, hugged Mom, and started to amble out with a, "I'll call you."

He was silent on the car ride, except when he connected his phone to my speakers, and one of those rap songs spilled out.

"What is this?" I immediately reduced the volume all the way through. "Jaja, I've told you I don't like these kinds of songs with foul language and naked women."

He rolled his eyes. "This is gospel rap. Be open-minded."

I grinned. "Yes. Roll your eyes at me. Shey, I'm the one who'll give you food. And you'll soon beg for money."

I had him there.

"Ah, ah. Sister, it's not like that now."

He smiled the smile that will have girls swooning in his class.

CHAPTER TWENTY-ONE

I hadn't heard from Alex since the text on Sunday. He'd been ignoring me at work and in church. I tried not to feel like a wallflower again and focused on the get-together, rather, the huge party Bianca was planning on my behalf.

I'd be confirming and re-confirming Modele and Simon's presence.

Bianca was running the show since she had the time, and my only job was to get the drinks which would be done on Friday evening so they'd be cold when my guests, or Bianca's guests, arrived. I didn't trust PHCN to cool them.

I didn't even know half of the people Bianca had invited. I kept getting texts from people confirming this and that. Since my only objective would be hopefully achieved, I wasn't really bothered.

Dad said he would be at the gym during the party, and since no alcohol would be served as it was basically a church party, Jaja could join in if he wanted. Or hang out in his room.

I'd already warned Bianca strictly that clean-up fell on her and her team of party planners. It was my only condition, which she heartily agreed to.

Already, the get-together—sorry, the huge party— was costing much more than I'd thought, but it wasn't a bother.

I realised I had a charmed life since I lived rent free and didn't even feed myself.

After I was done with fixing Simon up with Modele, then I'd focus on myself. After all, if I was going to progress and eventually get married, I'd need to get over Alex and be with someone else.

It was Friday, the day of the party, when I looked up from my desk to find Alex staring down at me. It was late. Everyone else had left, and I was trying valiantly hard to finish up before leaving for the weekend.

Why was he here?

"Am I invited to your party?"

"Of course. There's no guest list."

How had he found out? Oh. The news was everywhere. I'd sort of hoped my not formally inviting him meant he wouldn't show up. I couldn't stand to see him and Chioma all lovey-dovey in my house. Nope. But I couldn't out-rightly refuse to invite him.

He stood up, walked to the door, paused, then came back, a determined look in his eyes.

I looked into my screen quickly.

"What happened to us? I thought after our date at the restaurant, we'd be better friends. I feel like I did something to upset you, and you're avoiding me because of it. I just want to apologise. I know how sensitive you can be."

What? I raised my head up slowly, my sword drawn.

"Sensitive?" I basically said the word through gritted teeth.

He smiled. "Yes. You get too sensitive over little things. Or would you tell me what I did to upset you if I asked?"

No way in hell.

"See? That's what I mean. I've tried to be your friend, and you've rejected my friendship several times."

"You didn't do anything. We're friends."

"Prove it."

"How?"

"Have dinner with me. Now. You'll be too busy to eat during your party."

What?

"Ummmm, I'm busy."

He just raised an eyebrow in the way I love so much, and my heart tilted.

"I'm not lying. I do have to buy drinks for the party immediately after I leave here."

"Okay. We'll buy the drinks, then go out for a little bit. As friends."

And a small light in my heart dimmed. Of course. As friends. It's all he wanted from me. Friendship!

Why couldn't I just tell him I can't be friends with him?

'Cause you'll have to come up with a convincing lie, and we're not lying anymore, are we? Or are you bold enough to lay it all own?

And be vulnerable in front of him? No way. I know for a fact he's with Chioma. That would be a betrayal.

What if ...

There was no what if. He didn't like me that way, not anymore.

Coward.

I was not a coward. I just hated embarrassments.

I shut down my system, and we headed out to a drink distribution shop.

Alex stood beside me, and I gave them the list of drinks Bianca had come up with. The shop boy smiled.

"Madam, no alcohol?"

"No. Just give us these ones. How much discount..."

And so the haggling continued 'til we agreed at a price, and we stuffed the drinks into my boot.

By the time I headed back to make payments, Alex already had, and even though I felt a bit glad, chivalry and all, I couldn't argue.

Not that I didn't have the money to pay, but I do understand why it's so important he paid or offered to pay. I guess women in general just want a man who's comfortable with his wallet around them.

Anything other seemed to signify a certain lack of Knight in Shining Armor thingy.

And so, he led me to a restaurant suspiciously close to my house.

Did he know where I live?

Maybe he's stalking you.

No way. Why would he?

'Cause he's still into you ...

Ha!

I squelched the thought before my heart ran amok with it. It was hard enough sitting opposite him, watching him pore over the menu.

Gosh!

I loved him so much. It was pure torture to mask my feelings. Tears filled my eyes.

Why? Why can't you be mine?

"Are you okay?"

"Hmmmm."

Shit!

He'd seen my tears. I smiled nervously. "It must be the pungent smell of spicy food in here."

"I don't smell anything."

"That's because it's masked with air freshener."

We placed our orders, and the waiter moved away.

"So ... why have you been avoiding me?"

"I haven't."

He arched a brow.

"I really haven't."

He looked thoughtful. "I thought we would be ... after the date ..."

"What date?"

"Sorry, the dinner we had. I thought we would be closer as friends."

I smiled gratefully at the waiter as he dropped my order in front of me, and I dug in immediately. I was not having this conversation.

Alex took the cue and did not bring up any hanky-panky topic again. We surprisingly had a lot to talk about, and it was so easy to pretend we were on an actual date, that there was no Chioma in his life, and he was in love with me.

All too soon, we were done, and he drove off to go change for the party.

My house was literally crowded. I should have known. Bianca was not the right person to hand over your party to. She must have invited the whole church.

I quickly showered and changed into a breezy gown before heading to the living room where music was playing loudly and guests were scattered everywhere, laughing, dancing, or just talking.

And Simon was yet to get here, which left me bursting at the seams with anger. Kelechi, the drummer, had cornered Modele and been enthralling her with funny jokes for the past thirty minutes. They seemed to be having a really good time. Maybe he liked her, too.

No way. I wouldn't let him spoil my plans. I headed over to them and dragged Modele away with the pretext of helping me ensure everyone had a drink. She's so nice, she didn't even frown, and I started talking fast, about anything and everything I could think of, my eyes trained to the door, watching out for Simon.

I must have rambled so far off course that although Modele was smiling politely, I could see the question in her eyes. Luckily, Simon stepped in just in time, and I dragged her to him before he got bombarded by others.

"Why are you just coming now?" I hissed.

"Sorry. I had a flat."

"Wow. Hope you had a spare," Modele chimed in.

Simon smiled at her, and she smiled back. Good. Chemistry, right?

"I always have a spare."

"So you're always prepared. Like a boys scout."

"I was a Boys Scout."

Silence!

Why did they stop talking? Okay. Maybe they needed to get more comfortable. I cornered him to a vacant sofa and sat, gesturing to Modele to do same.

"So ..." and my mind went blank.

I virtually didn't know anything they might have in common. Oh, wait! I knew one thing; Church. "Service last Sunday was wonderful, right? I loved Pastor Lanre's message."

I hit Simon, who was busy peering into his phone.

"What? Oh, yes. It was good," he said absentmindedly and went back to his phone.

Great!

Was Simon just clueless, or was he really bad with girls?

OMG! Maybe that's why he's been single for so long. Modele was also peering at her phone, and of course, Bianca was gesturing wildly to me.

What, now?

"Don't go anywhere," I told Simon with a hard glint in my eyes.

Bianca grabbed my arm as soon as I got to her and started to pull me to the kitchen.

"We have an emergency."

"What happened? Did someone choke?"

She laughed. "No. This is more important."

She looked straight at me, like I should read her eyes. Honestly, what's up with her?

"The food won't be enough," she said with all seriousness, like the world was about to end.

I was not surprised.

"Really? You didn't realise that when you invited the whole church?"

"I didn't invite the whole church. Just a few of my friends."

"A few? I don't want to know what most or all of your friends would look like."

"So what do we do?"

Simon poked his head into the kitchen. "Can I see you for a minute?"

I turned to go.

"What about the food?" Bianca wailed.

"Handle it. It's your responsibility." I left her amid the pack of food, small chops, serviettes and more, looking confused.

"I'm tired of sitting with your friend. Please come and keep her company," Simon wailed.

"Where are you going to?"

"Everywhere." He stalked off.

Oh, no.

He must really be bad at talking to ladies. Maybe I should do more than introduce them. If I hint their good qualities to both, maybe their interest would spark.

Back at the sofa, Kelechi had wormed his way back to Modele, again, and they were laughing.

What was wrong with this drummer? I wouldn't let him spoil my plans.

I sat intentionally in their middle with my back to Kelechi. No matter how insane the topic was, he always found a way to butt in, right down to mascara types. Maybe he liked her.

Anyway, my plans were just getting ruined, and the night got worse.

I looked up, and there was Chioma, looking resplendent in a white ball gown, her make-up perfect, with strappy white heels and a dainty white bag.

Cinderella.

Perfect.

And who was the dashing knight standing beside her? Alex, of course.

Our eyes meet across the room, and for a moment, I couldn't hide the anger, the frustration I felt.

They were the perfect couple.

That old familiar bitterness tried to well up, and I closed my eyes and took deep breaths, running off to my room and shutting the door quickly.

Seconds later, there was a knock.

"Glory."

Alex. I couldn't let him see me with my mascara running down my face. Maybe if I stayed quiet, he'd go away.

"Glory, I know you're in there."

Shit!

"What ..."My voice came out croaked, and I cleared it. "What do you want?"

Just a little shaky. Good. Hopefully, he wouldn't notice.

"I don' t... I just ... are you okay?"

What did he care?

"I'm fine."

"Can I talk to you? This is ridiculous."

About what?

"I'll be out in a minute," I called out in what I hoped was a cheerful voice.

"I'm waiting."

"No. I'll come find you when I'm done."

Nothing.

Good. He was gone.

So I went about repairing the damage to my face. And when I opened my door, he was standing there, a knowing smile on his face. "You're .... You're still here?"

"I just want to .... I don't what to say or do anymore. Please help me out here."

I shrugged and casually leaned against the door. "There's nothing to say or do. I have to get back to the party."

"Dammit, Glory!" He pounded the wall.

Woah!

Maybe I should be getting upset, but I felt hot all of a sudden. Okay. Time to leave.

I spun across, and he held my hand.

"We're not through. You hear me, we're not through."

And he stalked off.

Wow!

The heat spread across my body and I quelled the urge to run after him, to hold his hands. Now, it was really time to leave. I headed into the living room, and Kelechi was still with Modele. Where the heck was Simon? Damn, I was swearing too much.

Great!

There he was, with the instrumentalists. Jeez. Didn't he care another man was hypnotizing his future wife—if all went to plan?

I stalked into the group, ignored their greetings, and pulled him away, which meant he willingly went with me because no way would I be able to pull him if he'd resisted.

"What is wrong with you?" I hissed.

"What?" He drained his can and dumped it into the trash can beside the door.

"You left Modele."

"I am not her babysitter. Besides, Kelechi has her occupied."

I jabbed my hands in his chest. "That is supposed to be your job."

He leaned against the door and looked at me with a calculating stare. "Why? Why is it my job to babysit her?"

I floundered. "Ummm, you know she can be very reserved. So ... I don't want her bored or alone."

He just kept staring, and I started to squirm.

"What?" I thundered.

"Nothing. I'll go be your babysitter." He stalked away, again.

Good.

"Thank you," I shouted to his back.

I left for the generator house, and there, in one of the columns, Alex and Chioma were sitting and talking, intimately.

Damn it! I didn't need this now. And it's how I found myself in Jaja's room, lying beside him while he played with his phone. I don't know how Bianca found me, but she knocked.

"Glory, everyone's leaving."

I had to say goodbye, be a good host.

I must be a good actress because nobody, not even Simon, noticed the coldness in my heart. The last guests, Bianca and her friends, left after the house was clean, and I retreated into my room.

It was final. I couldn't fight it anymore. I was in love with a man who was taken. My phone rang. Simon.

"Come outside," he barked and cut the call.

What did he want now?

I met him up beside his car outside my gate.

"Why do I get the sneaky feeling you're trying to set me up with Modele?" He went straight to the point.

"Because I think she will make a great wife. About this person you think you love, she just might not feel the same way about you. Have you thought about it?"

He looked intently at me. "Why would you think that?"

I took a deep breath and plunged in. "I know it's me, okay? I saw the love letter in your phone addressed to me, and I know. You're like my brother, Simon. We're great friends. Romance was never meant to be part of our friendship."

I dared to sneak a peek at him. His head was down, and his shoulders were shaking. Was he crying?

Oh, no. I ... He must love me very much. This was so difficult, and it was breaking my heart. "Don't cry, Simon. I'll always be your—"

Wait! Was he laughing?

He turned to me, and I saw him clearly as he burst into loud laughter, looking at me and hooting.

Uh! I was confused. What was funny?

"What? I saw the letter, the love letter in your phone addressed to me. I'm your wallpaper."

He managed to hold himself. "You should have asked. The letter was not for you. And you're my wallpaper because you did it yourself, and I haven't removed it because you're my best friend. *Capiche*?"

What?

"But ... It was addressed to me."

He brought his phone out. "Yes. To hide it from prying eyes. It wasn't for you."

Hmmm. So I wasn't the woman he's in love with. I felt relieved. "So, who is it addressed to?"

His grin faded. "None of your business."

He opened his door to get in, and I shut it with my foot.

"Simon Ferdinand Briggs, I am your best friend, and you will damn well tell me about this mystery woman you are in love with and obviously plan to marry."

He bent his head, took a deep breath, and looked at me. "It's Chioma."

What?

Chioma, man-stealer Chioma? To be sure, I asked. "Chioma in choir?"

"Yes."

Of all the... "Why didn't you tell me? How long has this been going on? I mean ... I don't understand. How could I not know?"

"I didn't realise it myself. I love her, and I'm going to marry her." He opened his door and got in. "Go inside. Try not to be as shocked as I was."

He drove off.

Chioma. First, she stole Alex, and now Simon? What did they all see in her, anyways? I was the one who should be getting all this love. Maybe not from Simon, but from Alex, at least.

What did she have that two great men were in love with her and none with me?

***

The following Saturday, I didn't even have the time to nurse my wounds. No.

I was angry and bitter, not just about the Chioma thing, even though the thought of her made me mad. It wasn't her fault my best friend and the man I love were all in love with her. No. That was just part of it.

My mom was the most ...

Oh, I couldn't even say it. How could she do this to my dad?

I didn't understand it.

Okay. It was going great. I'd managed to pull through rehearsals and ignore Alex's calls.

And just as I'd managed to escape, avoiding Chioma's friendly smiles, I got a call from my mom.

"Glory, get here now. Rabbit Hole."

Rabbit Hole? That's a restaurant.

I hopped into my car and rushed down there. The place was subdued, but just at the corner near the bar, I saw a small crowd gathered around a table. Somehow, I just knew.

There was my dad, with blood running down his nose, holding up his knuckles in obvious pain.

And there was my mom, holding a young, handsome man's hands, tears streaming down her face. She rushed up to me as she saw me.

"I don't know what happened. One minute I'm having dinner with Kunle, and the—"

"Who's Kunle?"

"Her new boyfriend," my dad growled, pointing to the man Mom was currently holding. His light complexioned face had an angry purple bruise in the shape of knuckles. My dad's knuckles, no doubt.

"What?" I yelled at my mom.

"No!" my mom shouts. "He's not my boyfriend."

"Really? You're lying now? Dinner in a restaurant, and you say he's not your boyfriend," my father retorts.

My mom gave him the hard eye. "He's just a friend, and we were just having dinner, not on a date. Which you rudely interrupted and punched Kunle."

Oh! This is the infamous Kunle.

"And I'll kill him as soon as this waiter leaves me alone." He glares at the waiter holding his arm and sticking his knuckles into an ice bucket.

"You won't kill anybody," Mom screams.

"Don't scream at him. This is all your fault." I glare at her as I go to my dad.

"How is it my fault? I was just having dinner."

"No. If you had talked to him like I asked you to, we wouldn't be here, would we?"

She floundered. "I'm trying…"

"Yeah. You're not trying hard enough."

I gave her my hard eye and helped my dad up.

He gave her a parting shot. "Maybe you can just try to remember you're a married woman. My wife."

She sat back down, next to Kunle.

"Yes. And remember, you're also a mother."

The drive home was silent as Dad left his car in the restaurant parking lot because of his hurting knuckles.

"You shouldn't have done that."

He grimaced and blew on his knuckles gently.

"I give up."

And it was the last thing he said all night. He just ambled into his room and closed the door.

Great! My mom was a jerk.

I so didn't like her right now. How could she do this to my dad?

CHAPTER TWENTY-TWO

My life was over. Dead. In fact, I didn't think I could show my face in church or at work again. Everything had just gone kaput. I mean, there was an embarrassing trending video of me on social media. How did this happen? Stupidity, if you ask me.

I had lost my friendship with Simon, Alex, and Chioma, and it was all my fault.

Well, most of it. I can't really blame myself. I'd been living with this dread Alex would engage Chioma soon. How did I come to that conclusion? Chioma said she had a dream about an engagement and that Alex had made plans for them at a high-end restaurant.

Alex himself had come up to me at work and asked, "What do you think about public engagements?"

My heart had skipped, died, then slowly come back to life. He was asking my opinion on how to propose to Chioma? I tried to be a good girl and let go. I tried to discourage him by asking, "What if she doesn't feel the same way and says no? You would just be embarrassed."

I know it was an evil thing to do, trying to stop another girl's engagement for my selfish interest, and I am not proud of it.

He just ignored me and said, "Oh, she'll say yes!" with a cockiness and arrogance I wish was directed at me.

"When is this engagement going down?" I asked, through tears lodged deeply in my chest.

"Today. You should come by. It's at VEROZ in GRA by seven." Then, he'd smiled at me, patted my head like a pet puppy, and walked away with a satisfied grin.

The insensitive jerk!

Don't blame him. Maybe if he knew how you felt, he might have asked you.

If only I could let him know I love him. What was this silence earning me, anyways? Pride? Who made the stupid rules that girls shouldn't let guys know they're into them unless asked? Why must it fall only to the guys? What stupid dignity were we trying to protect?

Calm down! Men are hunters. They don't like easy prey. The thrill is in the chase, and if he worked hard to get you, he'd value you more.

No way, Jose. I'd had enough. It was just a myth, right? After all, guys chased girls for months, years even, and lost interest after sex. I was going to tell Alex how I feel, and that's that. This dignity and self-respect would not keep me warm at night, and I didn't want to spend the next months or years nursing a broken heart, wishing I had at least tried all I could by telling him how I feel.

Besides, Simon was so certain Chioma would say yes to him, which meant she'd have to reject Alex, so I was just saving him from embarrassment. Yes. I had to save him from himself.

I felt strong, like a feminist crazy woman. Yes. Every woman should take control of her life and go after what she wants. Isn't that the definition of a twenty-first century woman? This is surely what feminism is all about, and even though I don't support all their ideals, I can use this one to my advantage.

I checked my watch. Almost six p.m. I had to hurry if I were to catch him before he entered the restaurant. I dropped all my files and rushed out. I should go home and change first, right? No. What if the proposal had already happened before I got there? No. I would wait in the parking lot and find a way to get Alex alone. Yes. That was good and fine.

Except ...

My back tyre went bust on my way there, and I had no idea how to change one. Don't look at me like that. I am not one of those take-charge women. I barely paid attention when my driving instructor was teaching me, and I had never needed to change my own tyre.

So I came down and realised I was in a deserted part of town. Very few cars passed by, and they all ignored me. Maybe the changing weather also wasn't helping. I'd stood for thirty minutes before I decided to try to change it myself. I couldn't leave my car out here, and my mechanic said it was raining heavily and he could only get to it in the morning. Hoodlums would steal my parts before he would get here the next day.

And that's how I found myself all dirty and greasy thirty minutes later when the rain poured down, and within seconds, I was soaked to the bone. Luckily, I had almost everything down pat, and I tightened the last screw and rushed into my car.

Oh, God! I couldn't go to the restaurant like this. I looked like a mad woman. I was completely soaked, my hair was standing up in spikes and clumps, my make-up had washed, and my mascara was running. Not surprising, the heel of my left shoe came off, and I had to go knock some sense into my engine before the car started.

The security guard at the restaurant gave me a suspicious look, and I ignored him and drove into an empty space. I saw Alex's car, and next to it was Simon's. Simon? Why was he here?

No, no, no.

I was too late. They'd gone in already, and Simon was obviously there. What if they both got into a fight over Chioma? The thought pushed me out of my car. I looked like a crazy woman, but there was nothing I could do about it. I had to save Alex.

I stepped into the foyer and walked into the restaurant when I saw the waiter pushing a cart of food. A tiny card on top of the dish read, 'Will you marry me?'

"Stop!"

But the waiter didn't hear me and was still wheeling the cart. I had to stop that cart before it got to their table. Already, I saw Chioma and Alex with his back to me, laughing and smiling intimately.

The waiter was already advancing, and just as she turned her head, I did the stupidest thing I had ever done.

I yelled, "Stop!"

But it didn't end there. No! Because I was running toward the cart, and my wet shoes on the polished floor lost their balance, and I was tumbling in the air ... and crashed into the cart.

Everything stopped for a while.

The hot bowl of rice was turned upside down on my stomach while the rice itself was on my head, pouring down my face onto my shoulders and into my bra. The cold glass of champagne dribbled down my thighs to my legs. I could feel thousands of eyes on me, murmuring. Somebody brought his phone out and took a picture, the light flashing in my hurting eye where grains of hot rice had stuck.

Then, I heard the familiar voice. Alex.

"Glory?"

Strange, but the voice was coming from behind me. Wait? Who was the man sitting with Chioma, then?

I raised my head and looked at Simon seated with Chioma. He was staring at me in shock. Maybe he didn't recognise me since I was covered in rice and drinks.

An arm helped me stand up, just as my other heel came off, and we crashed to the ground. Alex.

This time, Simon had recovered, and he helped us stand. "What's happening? Glory, what are you doing here?"

I wiped the rice off my face, and more dripped from my hair. I think one grain was in my nose.

I held Alex's hands. "I don't ... I came to tell you how I feel. You shouldn't marry her. You should marry me, you should love me."

"What?" Alex and Simon shouted at the same time.

A light flashed in my eyes, and I realised the entire restaurant was watching us. Some were taking videos. Well, I was already beyond embarrassed, so why not take the plunge?

Simon looked at me. "Are you drunk?"

I laughed. It's all so funny now.

"Yes. I am drunk, drunk in love with you, Alex. And I am tired of Chioma always getting what I want." I turned to her. "Why do you steal all the men in my life? I won't let you take Alex, you hear? I won't."

She looked at me with so much pity, and that teared me in. She sat there, so pretty and perfectly dressed up, pitying me for daring to lay it all out? As she opened her mouth to speak, I lunged right into her and started pulling at her hair. She screamed and grabbed my arm.

Simon pulled at me, and Alex tried to pry my fingers off her hair.

"It's just hair and make-up. I am as beautiful as she is. Look at her now ..." I say like a deranged harridan, proudly holding up the wisps of hair I had pulled off her.

They managed to tear me off her, and she looked at me in fear.

"That's right. Be afraid. Be very afraid, Chioma." I grinned like a maniac as Simon led her out of the restaurant and Alex dragged me away to the parking lot.

Simon whirled as soon as we were alone. "What is wrong with you? I have never seen such a show of reckless jealousy, insecurity, and violence. Why?"

"I already told you. I won't let Chioma have Alex. I love him." I turned to Alex. "I love you. I always have, and I tried to hide it, tried to tell myself I was lying, but when you said you were proposing to her, I knew I had to swallow my pride and tell you how I feel."

Alex looked at me, clenching his teeth in anger.

"You love me? I've been trying to get you to talk to me, to be a friend, but you've pushed me away time and time again. I thought we could revive what we had, but it turns out you're crazy. Why would you think I would propose to Chioma? She's my distant cousin, for crying out loud," he thundered.

"What?" I raised my head as a new fear entered my heart. "I would know if she's your cousin. She would tell me, you would tell me. I would know—"

"How exactly would you know?" Alex cut in. "You're just full of assumptions. If you bothered to ask me or your friend Chioma, you would know the only reason we've been spending so much time together is because she's been trying to help me win you back into my life."

Oh, no!

"And for your information," Simon said. "I was the one proposing to Chioma, not Alex. Alex is just here because I asked him to. If you were her friend, you would want her to be happy. You wouldn't try to steal her engagement. What kind of person are you?"

Chioma stopped sobbing so prettily for a moment and looked at me. "You should have told me. I would have ..."

She broke into soft, dainty sobs like a china doll, so of course, all the men led her to the car, and they drove away as I stood, dripping with shame and humiliation.

PART FOUR
The Peace

CHAPTER TWENTY-THREE

So, as you well know, coward that I am, I had been hiding my face in shame.

I refused to go to church on Thursday, and neither did I go for rehearsals. Alex had been avoiding me. The times we did run into each other, he looked at me with so much anger while I practically became a volcanic tornado of embarrassments. Videos of my episode had surfaced online. Luckily, they only got the part where I fell and the rice covered my face. I was now a gif. How wonderful.

Simon and Chioma had refused to pick my calls, and I was slowly going mad. I needed to apologize, to ease off some of the guilt I had been feeling, but they wouldn't let me. I don't know what came over me. How could I become so deranged and mad with jealousy and insecurity? I was not proud of my actions. Even if Alex had been the one proposing to Chioma, I had no right to be jealous or to try to stop it.

The worst part? I had seen a very ugly side of me, and I was not happy. I thought the blood of Christ was supposed to wash away all the ugly parts of a person?

Only when you allow Him and not your emotions.

Yeah, well, lesson learnt in the most painful and bitter way. Chioma had been putting up pictures of her engagement ring on Instagram. Apparently, Simon had taken her somewhere else and proposed after they'd left me. I was happy for them. Truly, I was. Now, I have nightmares Simon would never forgive me and I might not even get invited to the wedding, let alone being his Best

Man. Oh, God. He's my friend. I should be sharing this happiness with him. I missed him. I wasn't even angry he hadn't told me he about his proposal plans. I just wanted him back as my best friend.

Chioma, good girl that she is, hadn't told anybody of my deranged episode. At least, nobody had called to berate me. Nope. I did that pretty well to myself.

I had refused to think about Alex or what he'd said, else, I would just be a quivering mass of tears. Even thinking about it brought the tears to my eyes. How could I have possibly missed the fact Chioma was his distant cousin and he was trying to get me in his life again? How foolish could I possibly be? I should have known. Chioma had always been close to Pastor Lanre and his wife. What selfish friend have I been that I didn't even know she was a distant relation to Pastor?

I remembered bitterly all the times Alex had come up to me and tried to be a friend. What was I thinking at the time? The worst part? All this would have been avoided if I had been honest about my feelings instead of just assuming in my own little head. Assumptions! They will mess you up.

A Saturday without rehearsals just seemed a bit like I had been abducted by aliens, so I put on my gym clothes and went to the gym to ease off this restless energy. My dad had left a while back, and I wanted to see him doing some squats. That should make me smile.

Unfortunately, heading out to the gym led to another spiral.

It's not my fault or assumptions this time.

What else would I assume when I saw my dad lifting some weights with one bleached bimbo by his side, laughing and shoving her incredible bust into his face, flinging her hair every second, and wearing make-up? Who wore make-

up to a gym? Only man-chasing girls, and this one seemed
to think my dad was an easy catch. Trust me. I went up to
him, kissed his dimple, called him Daddy loudly, and gave
her the hard stare. She only giggled and left. Then, my dad
said he would call her and they would continue the talk.

So this was the point where I had to have the talk with
my dad, the uncomfortable talk where I had to warn him
some girls were only after easy money.

He was so glad to see me, so I picked one of the littlest
weights and start pretending to lift it.

"So, who's your friend?" I asked casually.

My dad smiled a goofy smile, and I got suspicious.
"Oh, that's Linda. She's my trainer, gym buddy, and
friend."

Oh! Gym buddies, huh. My dad can be gullible at
times. Case in point, these fake Aba gym sweats I currently
had on. Heck, I was so out of shape. Just this little weight I
was pretending to lift, and I was already sweating so
profusely. Of course, my fake sweats didn't absorb the
moisture, and I was getting uncomfortable.

"Just be careful, Dad." I grunt heavily. "Some girls
are not always so friendly."

He stopped and looked at me for a while. "Just what
do you mean by that?"

"Nothing. Just that some girls may want to take you
for a ride, especially now you may be single."

"Glory Okechukwu Owhor, I will not have you think I
am a moron when it comes to women. Linda is a friend, a
genuine friend I enjoy talking to. At least, she keeps me
company since your mother has abandoned me." He
grunted as he dropped the weight.

"Wait! You really think Mom is not coming back?" I
asked.

He snorted. "Your mother is pretty stubborn. I never thought she would leave me under any circumstance. What else do I think? Linda makes me happy, but I have no intention of making her your step-mother, so have no fear."

"What do you mean, she makes you happy? Are you dating this girl?" I glared at him.

"Your mother frolics around town with her boyfriend, and you think I will sit in the house and pine for her? No. Your mother may think I am a weakling, but I am a true African man." With that, he sauntered off.

I just sat for a while, too shocked to move. My dad dating or thinking of dating a young girl? What was the world coming to? Yet again, how could I blame him? Mom had left without any explanation, and the next thing, she was on a date with a younger man? Of course he would seek younger company to validate his manliness.

I will not have divorced or separated parents. I will not go through the hell of watching my parents with other people as they date or possibly get married again. No way.

It's how I headed out to Aunt Dorcas' to thrash it out with Mom. This nonsense must stop.

The security recognised me and let me in without announcing my presence. Which was a good thing because Mom was in the parlour, lying on the floor with Kunle, the same man from the restaurant, laptops and papers scattered everywhere, music from the speakers, and a bottle of wine and two glasses on the table.

I watched them for a while, and I noticed how free my mom's laughter was, how happy she seemed with her glowing face. There is something when you abandon your family. And I thought of Dad, the light that had left his eyes, how his steps had slowed and his shoulders had sunk, how he ate very little no matter how much I coaxed him.

So, of course, I exploded. Literally.

The best part was they didn't see me coming.

I first pulled my mom's arms and dragged her away from the young man. Then shouted in her face, and when the man touched me, I whirled on him and transferred all my anger and frustration on him. I yelled so much, my voice got hoarse.

And when I was done, I ended up on the floor, crying softly, spent. Why was I crying? Maybe the look of defeat on my dad's face, the loss of my best friend and Alex, the shame of my humiliation. I was crying for everything I had lost.

Then, I felt my mom's arms around me, which quietened me down.

It was silent, the evening bringing its cool breeze through the open door when she spoke.

"I got an offer to head an NGO targeted at bringing food and formulating education plans for thousands of homeless kids and orphans displaced by tornadoes, earthquakes, and other natural disasters all over the world. Your Aunt Dorcas arranged it all for me. It means I have to travel for months at a stretch. It's what I've always wanted to do. It's my last opportunity to do something else with my life, something meaningful except being a mother and a wife.

"Your father will never understand. He thinks I should be content with being his wife. But those kids, those hopeless eyes, call out to me. The statistics are staggering. So many of them end up as thugs, drug traffickers, and the girls head into prostitution. If diseases and crack don't kill them, gang violence does. They need this NGO, and I need this NGO. I didn't know what else to do."

She cleaned the tears in her eyes, her hands trembling slightly as I sat silent.

"That's why I left. Your dad would never allow me travel for months. I just … this is a dream come true, you know. It's what I have always wanted to do. I can't let this go. I may never have the opportunity again."

I shook my head and cleaned the mucus from my nose with my sleeve, relieved. "I understand. I really do. But you could have talked to me at least. You know Dad will support your decisions no matter what."

She scoffed. "He won't support it when he realises I would be gone for months at a time. I feel like I am abandoning my family, especially Jaja. He'll never understand."

I laughed. "Mom, I think you underestimate those who love you a bit too much. They may not understand or even like it at first, but if they love you, they'll support you. And I know for a fact Dad loves you."

She smiled sadly and sat on the back of her legs. "Yeah, I don't think so anymore. He so easily believed the worst about me. Kunle is an assistant from the NGO. He's teaching me everything I need to know."

"Mom …" I pulled her head up. "I know this means a lot to you, but do you really want to destroy your family to get it? Isn't there a better way you can achieve this? I am only asking because I am concerned for your marriage. Dad has a new girlfriend."

Okay, I exaggerated, but can you blame me?

And it worked. My mom's face squeezed in anger, and she looked at me with a thunderous expression.

"Who? Just a few weeks, and he has a girlfriend? Who is she?"

And she slid right down that hill where women blamed the mistress in their man's life and not the cheating man.

It was easy for her to follow me home, ranting all the way, bursting into tears at times, and me, I was just smiling. I had her hooked. As I got home, I sent her straight into their room while Jaja and I hauled the standing fridge against the door, then I sent a text. '*You guys are locked in there until this nonsense is settled.*'

Parent Trap-style right?

It didn't take long, anyways. My parents were such softies. By the next morning, they were all smiles, hugging and kissing, and Mom was in her old nightwear.

See? Life can be so easy. I make it complicated by living in my head and assuming stuff when I can just talk about it. Well, Nigerians are not known for talking, just aggression at any perceived slight.

Getting my parents back together left me with a healthy glow and an energy bubbling restlessly inside of me. I sat on the bed and tried to stop my knees from tapping aggressively. Then my hands started drumming on the bedsheet, and I found myself humming, exploding with joy. Automatically, I picked up the phone to call Simon, to tell him how awesome and smart I was, how I had single-handedly brought my parents back together. Then I remembered the Great Disgrace, and for that tiny moment, the sun in my heart dimmed, the pang of loneliness so sharp and acute. I knew what I had to do.

I headed over to Simon's, squelching down the heat and embarrassment making me want to turn back. By the time I drove into his compound, my heart was beating like I had just run a marathon race. Why was I shaking, anyways? It was just Simon—he had no choice but to forgive me. After all, he was my best friend; he was not supposed to make me sweat like this. Plus, I must have forgiven him countlessly over the years, and did I make him work for it? No!

The thought bolstered my courage, and I gloried in the spurt of anger that filled my chest, then knocked rapidly on his door, tapping my foot impatiently like one gearing for a fight.

When he opened the door, I entered into his spacious living room without a word and stood with my hands on my hips, still vibrating with anger.

He closed the door, sighed, and turned to me. "What?"

I saw red. "What do you mean by what? I am your best friend, Simon, or did you forget that part? You're supposed to love me despite my imperfections."

He just stood there, silently looking at me. It was like waving the red flag in front of the bull.

"Oh, so because you are now in love, you want to throw me aside, right?"

Simon sighed again in exasperation, rolling his eyes. "Is this supposed to be an apology?"

The fight left me. He was right. I had come to apologise in person, not to shout at him. "I'm sorry."

"What was that? I didn't hear you."

I said it again, louder. And looked up in time to see him smile. The pressure in my chest lifted, and I moved closer to punch his arm. "You jerk. You just wanted to make me dance, right?

When he smiled, the twinkle was back in his eyes. "Remember when you said you have never said 'I'm sorry' to anybody before? This was my chance, and I took it. You must love me so much."

I punched his arm again, and he yelled, rubbing his arm and glaring at me.

"It's what you get when you mess with me. But you know I really do mean it. I just—" deep breath. "—I went mad. Call it temporal insanity. It was like something possessed me, and I just couldn't stop myself. God!"

I covered my face from the embarrassment and flopped on the couch.

Simon sat on the single sofa. "That's what love does to you. It's irrational. Have you spoken to him? He was really upset that night. You just …"

My heart lurched, and I shook my head, recalling the tons of snivelling messages I had been sending to Alex, coupled with the fact he had refused to pick my calls, no matter how often or how late I rang.

"Let's not talk about him now. Why didn't you tell me you were in love with Chioma?"

I asked him the question that had been plaguing me. I was supposed to be his best friend. Yet, I'd had no clue.

Simon just shrugged. "Would you believe me if I say I have been in love with her for years?"

What?

He smiled at the look of surprise on my face. "Yes. I just didn't … anyways, I was lucky she wasn't taken."

"So …" I swung my legs back and forth. Now to another important question.

"So?" Simon replied with a straight face.

I groaned and rolled my eyes. "Do I even have to ask?"

"Ask what?"

"Don't play dumb. You know what I am talking about."

He raised his hands up innocently. "I don't know what you're talking about."

"I am still your Best Man, right?"

He looked at me, biting his lip as if thinking of something important. The tears started to rise. Had he already asked his younger brother who had been my sole contender all these years? He had always threatened to do exactly that in jest.

"You're not a man, Glory, so how can you be a Best Man? You're more of a Best Woman or Person."

The smile spread all across my face. And it's when I knew everything would be all right. I had acted abominably, but Simon's forgiveness meant I could finally forgive myself.

"... Besides, you were so brave that night, carrying a full plate of hot rice on your head and telling a man you love him. Biko, who told you that was the way to a man's heart?"

His shoulders heaved in laughter, and for the first time since it happened, I found myself laughing at my antics that day. What had I been thinking?

"If you had taught me how to win a man, maybe I would have done better. Honestly, you are a shitty wing man," I retort.

"Small me, teach you, the smartest of them all? It would be a sacrilege."

By the time I headed back home, my heart was light, the smile back on my face.

Well, all is well with my life, right? I didn't need love. Alex had refused to have anything to do with me, so I needed to move on. Guess I was too crazy for him. With time, hopefully, this gaping wound in my heart would heal.

With time, I will stop crying myself to sleep every night, or bursting into tears every time I hear a romantic song.

With time, my heart will not do its jiggy dance anytime I see him.

With time, the embarrassment will fade, and I will not torture myself with thoughts of what could have been if only I had just been a decent human being.

CHAPTER TWENTY-FOUR

Do you know how hard it is to plan a bachelor's night for your male best friend? It's Simon's wedding day, and I am completely exhausted. I can't wait for this day to be over. Even Chioma had taken me in as an unpaid wedding planner. Oh, I had travelled to buy souvenirs, bridesmaid materials, traditional attires and gears, drinks, and every other hullaballoo. But I can't complain. I know they're using my guilty conscience to get me to do stuff, but I don't mind.

Simon had promised to hold this over my head and even transfer the guilt to my first-born. I have promised my first-born I would work off this debt before they're born. I mean, Simon and Chioma had already forgiven me, and I had practically done everything for them, for crying out loud—I had been the one called in the middle of the night to pick up a lost bridesmaid from out of town and to find a matching lace the exact shade of pineapple blue. Pineapple blue?

Chioma had had a screaming fit when I'd told her there was nothing like pineapple blue in the market, so I had chucked myself up all around town, looking for pineapple blue. All the material sellers laughed me to scorn when I asked for pineapple blue that finally, I begged the tailor to send me a picture of the material and bought something close. I only hoped Chioma wouldn't notice 'til she was seated in church, or Hell would break loose. Who knew delicate, shy, endearing Chioma could become a bridezilla?

She had a perfect picture of what she wanted her wedding to look like, and God help anything or anyone who stood in her way. Everyone was afraid to speak up when she made unreasonable demands for fear of tongue-lashing. At least, she wasn't bursting into tears at any given time like my cousin Elda did. Elda burst into tears when dancing down the aisle, burst into tears when her mom danced in with her troupe of women, burst into tears when the cake designer was giving her speech, burst into tears when the food was being shared. I had never seen so much tears pour out of one tiny person in so little time.

Anyways, about the bachelor's night, Chioma made me promise not to let any girl/stripper near her husband-to-be, and all of Simon's friends groaned when I announced it would be held at a bar down the road. So I got hijacked into the vehicle and the driver, a groomsman, completely ignored my directions and drove us to a spritzy club in GRA. We were ushered in by girls in feathery lingerie, but I pulled the line when they brought a dancer to our table. I mean, Simon and I at least are born again. I know. They called me buzz kill, but who cares? I also didn't let the party last more than an hour, and then, we went back to the hotel and slept soundly. At least, I did. I had a sneaky feeling some of the groomsmen had snuck out afterwards back to the club.

Anyways, here I was, barking orders at the serving girls and discouraging women with bowls from lining up the buffet stand where the food was being served when, of course, Alex walked in, so blindingly handsome, I almost failed to see the lovely, light-skinned girl in a very tight dress and incredibly thin heels hanging on to his arm. I looked down at the suit and bow tie I was required to wear as the Best Man and cringed. My hair was a short Rihanna style to fit in with the groomsmen. Gosh. Could I look any more dorky?

They smiled and headed over to a table, and he pulled out a chair for her to sit. That's when I got angry. It had been three months—three months where I had apologised endlessly, but he'd ignored my calls and hadn't replied my messages. The cheek of it. At work, he was so cold, I had delegated all Alex-related work to Juliet. As if all that was not enough, he'd had the audacity to bring a girl here?

To show you he's over you.

Fine. If he wanted to play, then two could play that game. I turned and smiled my blinding smile at the handsome man who had been staring at me all day. He was dressed smartly, with some other guys from Simon's office. He smiled back and stood up, walking towards me.

I would show Alex how I, too, had moved on. After my shameful debacle, I had no pride, no dignity left, and even after all my apologies, he still held a grudge and came here to undermine me? No way. I would play this game, and I would win.

Mr. Handsome introduced himself as Eric, and we hit it off. He led me back to his table and introduced me to his friends. I laughed over everything he said, touched his arm generously, and gave him my number when he asked. I looked towards Alex, and I smiled within at the way he was frowning at me. Whatever.

Eric offered me a glass of wine, and I downed it in one gulp, never mind how I hadn't had alcohol in years. I needed to forget this dull ache in my heart. I needed to move on. Alex was not God. I had embarrassed myself too much over one man, and it was time I had a bounce back.

But you're using fire to cure fire.

Whatever. Eric would understand when I became cold after today. He seemed like a smooth player. Just what I needed, someone to make me feel less lonely while Alex caroused with his new girl.

Simon's mom called for me when it was time to share souvenirs, and soon, my hands were full with the bag of plastic bowls and tiny clocks as I handed them out. Stoic, I got to Alex's table and handed two souvenirs to the girl he'd come with. He just glared at me, then held my arm when I turned to leave.

I glared right back at him. "What?"

"I want to talk to you."

I laughed scornfully. Talk? I'd been begging him to talk to me for three months. "No chance in hell."

I slipped right out of his hands and continued handing out souvenirs to the next table. Oh, the gall of it. After ignoring me all along, never mind the embarrassing, awkward, and stilted office conversations and how skilfully he'd managed to avoid me in church, now he wanted to talk?

I had said my piece, done all the apologising I could do, and I had made my peace with it. No way would I dig up painful memories. Obviously, he had moved on. I would not shamefully declare my love for him again. Never. He wasn't such a gentleman, after all, letting me take all the heat and never once seeking to help me restore my dignity. Who does that? A simple 'apology accepted' wouldn't have killed him.

By the time we finished sharing souvenirs, Simon had given his speech, and the hall started to empty out. The gifts were being loaded into a van, and I left one of the groomsmen to oversee it all while Simon's mom took me round to introduce me to her friends. Chioma and her friends were dancing at the stage, and the decorator had started taking off the chair covers when I got a chance to sit and look at my phone. It was finally over. Simon was married and now had a new best friend.

He'd never be always so available for me anymore. It's great, but I was going to miss the closeness of our friendship. He was my only friend—the rest were colleagues at work or choir members in church whom I rarely saw outside of the circle. I was completely alone again.

Where was this loneliness coming from?

"Are you alright?" Eric was standing before me.

I smiled and stood up. "That was my best friend. Now, he has a new best friend."

He smiled at me. "I can be your new best friend, if you want."

He meant it.

"Let's just be normal friends and see how it goes."

He sat next to me and looked at his phone.

"Your friends are leaving. Won't you leave with them?" I asked.

"I'll drop you off anywhere you want," he said, then went back to his phone.

This simple act of kindness did me in, and tears sprung into my eyes. Gosh! What was wrong with me? Had I been without human contact for so long that this random act of kindness did me in? I stood up hurriedly and headed to the ladies' where I stared at the tears as they welled up and rolled down my face.

I needed a boyfriend, a husband. I needed somebody in my life. It was time to let go of this self-imposed barrier and finally be with somebody, somebody whom I'd have all to myself, who would care for me in that special way no one else can. Maybe Eric could be that person.

And Alex?

I would not even dignify this with a response. Okay, my job was done. My heels were killing me, so I just needed to get my slippers from the boot of the car that had brought us here and go home with Eric.

But Eric was not the person standing outside the bathroom like a stalker. Nope. It was Alex. What, now?

"What? You've come to get another apology in person? Leave me alone," I practically screamed.

His face hardened. "We need to talk."

I scoffed. "There's nothing to talk about. I begged you to talk to me, and you refused. You watched me sink to an all-time low, and you never even bothered to check on me or try to make me feel forgiven. No. You let me stew in guilt for so long. Well, I've had it up to here. I know what I did was wrong, but what you did was worse. You've had your fun. Now let me pass."

He stalked towards me, and I slipped past his side and ran out into the hall, straight to Eric.

"I'm ready. Let's go."

He smiled and held my arm as he led me to the parking lot. It was late evening, and the sun was already going down. It was almost dark. His car was a Toyota Prius, and he held the door for me and I got in, then he walked around to his own door.

That's when my door got torn open abruptly and an arm reached in and dragged me out.

Alex.

He looked so angry, for a moment, I remembered those dark days in school when he used to be violent. But he just dropped my arm as soon as I was out of the car.

"I'm sorry," he said.

Eric got down and came to me. "Who is this? Are you okay?"

He held my arms and looked at me from head to toe.

Alex growled, and I knew he was really upset.

"Don't touch her," he yelled at Eric who promptly put me behind him and looked at Alex, taking a defensive stance.

Men!

Always big show-offs.

"It's okay. No need to fight. He's my friend."

Of course, they ignored me.

"Who are you?" Eric asked again.

Alex scowled and tried to grab me from behind Eric. "I am her boyfriend. Glory, come out of there and—"

Eric pushed him away. "She doesn't want to go with you."

"Hello?" I said, but of course, my voice was lost in this show of manliness. It would be so comical if not for the fact I was worried they might actually get into a fight. I would have burst into laughter otherwise.

"Listen, Glory is my girlfriend. We had a little fight, and she's upset with me. But she is not leaving with you," Alex said through gritted teeth.

'Well, she says she's not your girlfriend." Eric smiled like he was enjoying this.

The girl Alex had come with walked up to him and held his arm, whispering gently into his ear, and my heart curled.

"Yes ... Go to your new girlfriend and leave me alone," I yell from behind Eric, then make to open the door.

I heard a grunt and felt a sudden gust of wind behind me, and by the time I had turned around, Alex had shoved Eric away, and he looked mad.

Okay. I needed to stop this.

"Alex, stop this nonsense. This is not who you are anymore."

He looked at me, so intense, so completely honest, my heart actually lurched in me.

"I know, Glory, but I just need to apologise, and ..."

I could see Eric had gotten his balance, and he looked like an enraged elephant, so I quickly stepped in front of Alex and held Eric's arm.

"He is ... was my boyfriend. I have to go with him." He looked ready to protest, so I quickly added, "I'll call you. Okay?"

He smiled, nodded, and headed to his car while I glared at Alex until Eric had driven off.

"Now, what do you want?" I asked briskly.

The girl beside him walked away, and I shook my head. "Where's your girlfriend going to?"

'She's not my girlfriend. She's my cousin. Another distant cousin."

"You must have them in dozens," I scoffed.

"I just want to apologise. I'm sorry, I was a fool. I should have been flattered and happy you loved me enough to make such a public scene. It's one thing I've always admired about you. You can be very reserved, but once you believe in something, you don't let anything stand in the way. Me? I'm just a coward, a big one. I should have hugged you, I should have ... I respect what you did that day."

"And yet, you've been avoiding me. You act all supercilious and make me feel like a love-struck idiot. I wasted my emotions on you, Alex, and you were not even man enough—"

"I know, and I am truly sorry." He knelt down, and passers-by started to stand and stare.

My cheeks grew hot with embarrassment. "Stand up."

"No. You were not ashamed to make a fool of yourself for me, so I have to return the favour. I love you, Glory, and I know I don't deserve a strong, beautiful woman like you."

I held his arm and led him away from all the stares and interested matrons looking with disdain and a flash of jealousy. Yeah, I know. It's not every day a guy kneels for a girl in public in Nigeria. Whatever.

I ignored the rush of joy thumping through my chest or the hotness of my cheeks or even my heart as it screamed "Yes" over and over again.

We were seated inside the hall where a woman and two boys were striping down the decorations from the walls, table, and chairs.

Alex sat beside me, and his hands were trembling slightly. I suddenly remembered the day we officially got together in school, and I smiled widely. *Oh, my Alex, how I love you so.*

When did I become such a gushy female?

Alex held my hands and looked into my eyes, and I was spellbound; I couldn't move. He was so perfect, and now, I was trembling and shy. I looked down, but he raised my face with his hand and kissed me softly on my lips. That's when I started shaking. I wanted more, but he just looked at me and started talking.

"It was my fault we lost touch when I travelled out. I got so caught up with school and activities, and I felt you weren't making any effort, either, so you must have found a new guy or guys. Glory, I am an intensely jealous person, and I have an active imagination. I came back, and there you were, right in my church, but it seemed like you had forgotten me, and even when it seemed like you hadn't, I thought you were dating Simon."

I shook my head and started to protest, but he placed his finger on my lips to hush me. Was it bad how I wanted to lick his finger? And why wasn't he kissing me again?

Glory, concentrate. After his speech, maybe more kisses for you.

I shook my head and tried to focus on what he was saying.

"… even if you were with him. It drove me crazy, and sometimes, I just wanted to tear you away from his car and take you to my house and lock you up."

Why didn't you do it?

But I couldn't speak. His finger was still on my lips, and I was trembling with the ache to rub my lips all over it.

"Chioma wasn't sure you two were dating, and she was having feelings for Simon. So, we became heartbreak buddies, pining after the ones we want together. What I truly regret is leaving you to feel awful for months after the proposal debacle. It warms my heart that you would go to such lengths for me, but I was scared, scared you were only picking me as second choice after Simon. I wanted you to love me with the same intensity I love you, and …"

Trust me.

I removed his hand, barely said, "I love you, too," before I kissed him with all the hunger inside of me.

Damn!

His lips were still the softest ever.

EPILOGUE

I have a new best friend. Good thing is, he's also my fiancé. Yes. He proposed, and I said yes.

I'm still a very boring wallflower. Just ask Alex. I'd rather stay indoors reading novels or watching movies all the time than hang out with anyone. He has to literally force me out of the house occasionally.

As for my parents, they're back to being all lovey-dovey. It's hard to be without my mom for months, and it will get even harder when I leave. So, Mom got Aunt Dorcas to contact a trusted agency for House Assistant interviews when she gets back this time. She doesn't like the term housegirl/boy or househelp. The House Assistant would help my dad and Jaja with some mundane tasks when Mom goes on her trips.

I've decided, after all this debacle, to stop living in my head, to stop assuming, to start speaking. It's still difficult to make friends easily, especially now that I have a new best friend, but I am making the effort. Modele and Bianca actually came to my house for a sleepover.

I know we're too old for stuff like that, but it has been a fantasy, and I managed to bribe them. Don't ask me with what. Just don't be too surprised if you see two strange faces reading you.

Thank you, diary, for listening to all my woes. I hope I didn't bore you too much.

Thank you for reading Diary of a Wallflower.

If you enjoyed this story, please leave a review.

ABOUT GLORY:

Glory Abah is a die-hard romantic whose head has always been in the clouds. She started reading books from a very young age and finally, decided to pen down the love stories she fantasizes about. She lives in Nigeria and loves to hear from her readers.

Join her mail list to have first access to free stories, book releases, discounts and many more exciting offers, including a FREE book.

CONNECT WITH GLORY

Facebook: https://www.facebook.com/gloryabahpage/

Twitter: https://twitter.com/gloryabah

Instagram: https://www.instagram.com/iamgloryabah/

Mailing list: http://eepurl.com/dnpV-r

OTHER BOOKS BY LOVE AFRICA PRESS

His Captive Princess by Kiru Taye
Love at First Sound by Amaka Azie
Dawsk by Erhu Kome Yellow
Unravelling His Mark by Zee Monodee
Love and the Lawless Anthology by Emem Bassey, Onyeoma Izunna, Julie Onoh, Obinna Obioma and Kiru Taye

CONNECT WITH US
Facebook.com/LoveAfricaPress
Twitter.com/LoveAfricaPress
Instagram.com/LoveAfricaPress

www.loveafricapress.com

LOVE AFRICA
PRESS
African Love Stories

CPSIA information can be obtained
at www.ICGtesting.com
Printed in the USA
LVHW091454161221
706294LV00010B/1109